Suddenly, Chris grabbed my arm and yanked me back into the doorway of a shoe store.

"What the—" I began.

"Look who's over there," she said, pointing across the way. Standing in front of the record store was a very cute boy. He was tall with dark hair.

"Isn't he in the ninth grade at school?" I asked. Then I remembered. "I know. He's Kim Swanson's boyfriend."

Kim Swanson is a girl in our eighth–grade class. She's not someone I'm particularly wild about, but I guess you'd have to say she's one of the coolest kids in our grade.

"His name is David Madison," Chris informed me in a tone of deep admiration.

"Why are we hiding from him?" I asked.

"I don't want him to see us watching him," Chris said.

I was getting worried about Chris. Was she losing her mind?

ALL ALONE
IN THE
EIGHTH
GRADE

Suzanne Weyn

Cover by Bruce Emmett

Troll Associates

Library of Congress Cataloging-in-Publication Data

Weyn, Suzanne.
  All alone in the eighth grade / by Suzanne Weyn.
    p.   cm.—(Midway Junior High)
    Summary: Twelve-year-old Tracey fears she is losing her best
friend Chris when Chris gets her first boyfriend and becomes a part of
the popular crowd at school.
    ISBN 0-8167-2394-X (lib. bdg.)   ISBN 0-8167-2395-8 (pbk.)
    [1. Friendship—Fiction. 2. Schools—Fiction.] I. Title.
II. Series.
PZ7.W539A1 1992
[Fic]—dc20   90-10162

A TROLL BOOK, published by Troll Associates

Printed in the United States of America.

10 9 8 7 6 5 4 3 2

ALL ALONE IN THE EIGHTH GRADE

To Tara Muzio, a shining star.

CHAPTER

$\mathcal{S}$ome changes you see right away. Others just sort of sneak up on you. My best friend, Christine Kirk, might have been changing in small ways for a long time. But I didn't notice—at least not until one Saturday afternoon at the end of September. From that day on, though, I knew she wasn't the same Christine I had grown up with.

My first clue that something was up came when Chris didn't want to watch a video with me that Saturday afternoon.

We had been watching a video every Saturday for the last two years. And I even had a copy of *Mutant Killer Termites*, which I'd had to reserve a week in advance. I love horror movies—nothing beats that great, tingly feeling of being scared out of your wits. Chris loved them, too. Or at least I always thought she did.

"This movie is supposed to be so cool," I said as I slipped the tape into Chris's VCR. "I heard the scene where Johnny Dupré battles the mutant termites is completely awesome." I'm a big fan of Johnny Dupré. He's in lots of horror movies. The only thing better than watching a scary movie is watching one with a really hunky-looking guy running around saving everybody.

The FBI warning was still on the screen when Chris stood up in front of the set. "Tracey, do you mind if we don't watch this right now?" she asked.

I did mind. I'd been looking forward to seeing the movie all week. "Why not?" I asked.

"I kind of wanted to go to the mall today," she said. "My contact lenses came in. They said I could pick them up any time."

"Your *what* came in?" I shrieked, hitting the pause button on the VCR. Chris had worn thick glasses since the fifth grade. I had no idea she was getting contacts.

"I decided to get contact lenses." Chris tugged nervously on a piece of her long blond hair.

"Why didn't you tell me?" I asked.

Chris shrugged her slim shoulders. "I don't know. I was afraid you might think it was silly."

"That's not exactly the kind of thing you can hide from a person. Didn't you think I'd notice you weren't wearing glasses?" I asked.

"Don't get insulted," said Chris defensively. "I just told you about the contacts right now, didn't I?"

She was right. I was insulted. Chris always told me everything right away. Normally she would have asked my opinion about contacts. Then she'd have wanted me to help her convince her parents to let her get them. I would have been in on the entire process from the first second it popped into her head until the moment she popped the lenses into her light blue eyes.

But I wasn't.

This should have been my second clue that things were changing between us.

"So, are you going to come with me?" she asked.

I snapped off the VCR. *Mutant Killer Termites* would have to wait. "Of course I'm coming," I said, grabbing my denim jacket. "I can't believe you didn't tell me about this."

Chris lives five blocks from the mall, so getting there was no problem. As we walked along Lee Street, I sensed that Chris had something on her mind. She was naturally a quiet person, but not around me. Today she hardly said anything.

"Is something the matter?" I asked.

Chris stuck her hands in the pockets of her jeans. "Do you think I'm a geek?" she asked.

"That's a totally dumb question," I told her. "Of course you're not a geek."

"Think about it," she said. "We're in the eighth grade and neither one of us has ever had a boyfriend."

"Johnny Myers had a mondo crush on you last year," I reminded her.

"*Eeeewww.*" Chris winced. "That doesn't count."

Okay, so Johnny was extremely fat and always smelled like dirty socks. But he *was* a boy.

"I could have gone out with Tony Armand this summer," I said.

"But you didn't want to. That just proves my point," said Chris. "I mean, maybe we *are* geeks and we don't even know it."

"Hold on," I said, annoyed. "What is this *we* business? Tony is nice but I just didn't feel all lovey-dovey about him. You can call yourself a geek—even though you're not. But leave me out of it. I like myself just the way I am."

This was mostly true. I mean, nobody likes themselves completely. I wish my hair were red and curly, instead of brown and wavy. Still, I'm pretty happy being me.

I looked at Chris. Maybe the thick glasses *did* have a slightly geeky look to them, but they were on their way out. The rest of her seemed fine. She had a pretty face, and she was a full two inches taller than I. Chris was just an average, normal girl.

"It's okay for people to change, don't you think?" Chris went on. "Just because you've been one way all your life doesn't mean you have to stay that way, does it?"

"I guess not," I admitted. I hadn't really thought about any of this before.

Apparently Chris had been thinking about it a lot. Something had to be behind it. "Did anything happen? Did someone in school insult you or something?" I asked.

Chris shook her head. "No. Nothing like that happened. But don't you sometimes wish you were really cool and that all the boys liked you?"

"I suppose," I replied. "But the kids in school like us well enough."

"It's not the same as being really popular," Chris disagreed.

We arrived at the Greatdale Mall and took the escalator up to the second level. Chris was so excited she practically ran to the Eye Center. "Slow down," I called as I hurried after her.

Inside the store, the optician took Chris into an examination room in the back to make sure everything was okay with the contacts. When she came out, her eyes were a dazzling, deep shade of cornflower blue.

"I didn't realize you were getting tinted lenses," I said, surprised.

"I love them! Do you like them? I love them!" she babbled excitedly, gazing at herself in the mirror. "I feel like a whole new person. They're so beautiful. What do you think?"

What did I think? I thought they looked kind of pretty, but phony. Her eyes reminded me of a movie I'd seen. People's minds were being taken over by creatures from another planet. You could tell who the creatures had gotten by this weird look in the people's eyes. I bet the actors wore tinted lenses in the movie. Their eyes just weren't the color of real eyes.

"They look great," I said. I didn't want to stomp on her happiness by telling the truth. What good would that have done? "I like your regular eyes, but these are nice."

"Nice?" she cried. "They're gorgeous!"

Outside the Eye Center, Chris stopped and examined her reflected image in a store display window. "I hate my hair," she commented critically. "I need a new haircut."

"I think it looks okay," I said. "Maybe you could just use a trim."

Diagonally across the mall was Happy Scissors Unisex Haircutters. "Come on," said Chris, running on ahead. I caught up with her in front of their sign. "I have some money left from the lenses. And I have my baby-sitting money." She pulled some crumpled dollar bills from her pockets. "I have twenty-five dollars."

"Saturday Special," I read the sign. "Haircut and blow-dry, only ten dollars."

We stepped into the haircutters. "Go see Yvette, chair sixteen," the woman at the front desk told Chris.

The chairs were marked and we counted down to sixteen. All along the walls were pictures of men and women in different hairstyles. "I love the way she looks," said Chris, pointing to a picture on the wall. A pretty woman with white-blond hair modeled a very layered haircut with wispy bangs all around her forehead and face. "Do you think my hair would look good like that?" Chris asked me.

I tried to visualize that hairdo on Chris. "I don't know," I replied skeptically. "I don't think it's really you."

Chris frowned. "Oh, you mean I should get something geekier."

"Christine!" I exploded. "Cut it out with this geek stuff, would you? Get the stupid haircut if you like it. I don't care."

"It just bugs me when you say something isn't me," Chris snapped. "It's like *me* has to always be the same or you're not happy."

"I like you the way you are," I said. "Is that so terrible?"

Chris shoved me lightly on the shoulder. Then she stuck out her tongue and crossed her eyes. I made the same face back at her. It made both of us laugh. Ever since we were little that was the way we got out of an argument. It was like a silly signal that the fight was over.

At that moment a small, thin woman with short, spiky blond hair came over to the chair. She wore tight black stretch pants and a large white top with sparkly designs on it. "Hi, girls. I'm Yvette. What can I do for you today?" she said.

"I'd like that," said Chris, pointing at the picture on the wall.

"You want the color and the cut?" asked Yvette.

Chris turned to me and I didn't like the look in those blue-blue eyes. They were a little too wide with excitement. "Chris, you can't bleach your hair!" I said. "For one thing, you don't have enough money."

"Styling, color, and blow-dry is thirty dollars," Yvette told us.

"I almost have it," Chris insisted. "How much have you got on you?"

"Ten," I admitted reluctantly. Unfortunately I had just baby-sat for Mrs. Liebowitz the night before. Normally I don't have that much money in my pockets.

"Okay," Chris told Yvette before I could say another word. "Give me the color and the cut. I want to look just like her."

I looked to Yvette and hoped she would try to talk Chris out of it. After all, Chris had only just turned thirteen.

Yvette squinched up her eyes and cocked her head as she studied Chris. "Totally adorable," she concluded after a moment. "The color will boost your whole look. And since you're a blonde anyway, the roots won't be a big deal for you."

In no time, Yvette was pouring purplish stuff all over Chris's head. Then Chris had to wait for half an hour. "What is your mother going to say?" I asked as she thumbed through a fashion magazine.

"She'll freak, probably," Chris replied coolly.

"Doesn't that worry you a little?" I asked.

"Yeah, sure, but how mad can she really get? It's not like I murdered somebody, or cut out of school or anything. It's *my* hair. She'll be mad for a while. Maybe she'll even ground me. But when it's over, I'll have the hair I want."

I was stunned. I had never heard Chris talk like this. She always used to worry about getting into trouble. It was becoming obvious to me that she was completely serious about changing her image.

When Chris stepped out of Happy Scissors Unisex, I hardly recognized her. I had to admit, though, she did look great.

"Those pants Yvette had on were cool, weren't they?" Chris commented.

"Don't look at me," I said. "You used the last of my money when you tipped Yvette."

"I know," said Chris. "Guess what Yvette told me while she was washing my hair? Her real name is Gladys. She changed it to Yvette."

"Oh, no!" I wailed, covering my face with my hands. "I can't take anymore. Please don't tell me you're going to change your name!"

"I wasn't," Chris said with a slight pout. But I could tell from her expression that she had been thinking about it. What was with her?

Suddenly, Chris grabbed my arm and yanked me back into the doorway of a shoe store. "What the—" I began.

"Look who's over there," she said, pointing across the way. Standing in front of the record store was a very cute boy. He was tall with dark hair.

"Isn't he in the ninth grade at school?" I asked. Then I remembered. "I know. He's Kim Swanson's boyfriend."

Kim Swanson is a girl in our eighth-grade

class. She's not someone I'm particularly wild about, but I guess you'd have to say she's one of the coolest kids in our grade.

"His name is David Madison," Chris informed me in a tone of deep admiration.

"Why are we hiding from him?" I asked.

"I don't want him to see us watching him," Chris said.

I was getting worried about Chris. Was she losing her mind?

"Patty Handleman told me that Kim doesn't really like him anymore. She must be insane. But that's good news for me," Chris continued.

"It is?" I asked, confused. "Why?"

"Because then he'll be available," she said, as though the answer should have been obvious.

"Available for what?"

Chris's new blue eyes took on a dreamy expression. "Available for me," she said.

CHAPTER 2

Two weeks went by. It was almost mid-October and Kim Swanson still hadn't broken up with David Madison. "Are you sure you got the story right?" I asked Chris as we walked down the hall of our school, Midway Junior High.

"Yes, I got it right," insisted Chris in an irritated voice. "Patty Handleman says that Kim doesn't want to hurt David's feelings, but she's definitely looking for the right moment to break up with him."

"How does Patty know all this stuff?" I asked.

"Patty is Phyllis Mann's cousin. And you

know that Phyllis and Kim are very tight," Chris explained.

I laughed and shook my head. "Patty is like your personal spy."

"Yeah, I'm lucky that she tells me stuff," Chris agreed seriously, not seeing anything funny about it.

"Still, Chris, don't you think you ought to give up on David?" I suggested. "I mean, he's not the only boy in school. And you don't even know him."

I hated to see Chris setting herself up to be disappointed. David didn't even know she was alive.

Plus, I had my own reasons for wanting her to forget about him. Ever since the day she'd gotten her contacts, Chris had continued to change more and more. She started wearing this heavy blue eyeliner and purplish mascara. Her nails were always painted. As soon as she saved up the money, she got herself a pair of black stretch pants like the ones Yvette had worn.

It wasn't just her looks that were changing, either. For one thing, all she ever wanted to watch now were rock videos. And she was more interested in what people were wearing or the way they moved than anything else. It was as if she was studying them.

At least she hadn't changed her name to Yvette. Not yet, anyway.

22

I kept hoping that once she realized her crush on David was hopeless, she would go back to being the Christine Kirk I once knew. Because, for all her weirdness, I still considered Chris my best friend. I mean, when you've been best friends with someone since first grade, you don't just give it up because the person falls in love and goes a little screwy on you. Friendship is a much deeper thing than that.

Her crush on David *was* hopeless. He was in the ninth grade and there was really no way to meet him. The only eighth graders he hung out with were Kim's friends. Those kids were generally considered to be super cool. And though Chris and I were not geeks, I guess you would have to say we were not super cool, either.

But Chris was certainly working on it.

"Guess who asked to look at my history notes yesterday," said Chris. "Phyllis Mann."

"That's nice," I said. "So what?"

"Phyllis never used to even talk to me. But a lot of kids from Kim's crowd have noticed how much I've changed. I think I'm really starting to be accepted by them."

"Excuse me if I don't drop dead with joy," I said drily.

"You're impossible!" cried Chris. "Do you want to go through the rest of junior high and high school being part of the out crowd?

Besides, the only way I'll get to meet David is by being friends with Kim's friends."

"Maybe you wouldn't even like David if you got to know him," I pointed out.

"I would like him," Chris assured me. "Every time I look at him my hands shake. I think about him all the time. I dream about him."

I glanced at the cover of Chris's notebook. She had scribbled the name David so many times and in so many different ways that it completely covered the book. She had it bad, all right.

As we continued down the hall, we neared Kim's locker. As usual, a whole group of kids was hanging around it. There were Phyllis Mann, Jessica Arnold, Gloria Chen, and Matt Herman. In their midst was Kim Swanson. Wispy layers of soft blond hair framed her face. Her dark-lined eyes were pale blue. Kim exuded coolness without saying or doing much. It occurred to me that maybe saying and doing little *was* the secret of coolness.

"Hi!" Chris waved brightly to Phyllis Mann.

"Hey, Chrissie, Tracey," Phyllis responded. As Kim's friends went, Phyllis was one of the nicest. And she had beautiful red curly hair, just the kind I wanted. Other than that, I didn't know very much about her, even though we were in a few classes together.

Chris wasn't about to let this opportunity

slide by. She scurried right over to the group. I didn't want to stand there like a dope, so I followed.

"I adore your earrings!" Chris told Phyllis. Phyllis's earrings were pretty blue stones stacked on top of one another. From the tone of Chris's voice, you would have thought they were Princess Di's royal jewels.

It did the trick, though. Phyllis started telling everyone all about the trip she'd taken to the Bahamas and a boy she'd met there who'd bought her the earrings. Chris had found just the right thing to comment on. Or, more likely, Patty Handleman had tipped her off.

Matt Herman said good-bye and all the girls started listening to Phyllis's story. Just when she got to the part where the boy asked if he could come visit Phyllis at Christmas, the bell for first period class rang.

"I *have* to know how this story ends!" cried Chris as though this were the most fascinating story she had ever heard.

"Old man Harmon will have me in detention again if I'm late for class," said Kim in her throaty voice. Without waiting for anyone, she headed slowly on down the hall. For someone worried about detention, she didn't seem in a rush. She *was* cool.

"I'll tell you the ending at lunchtime," said Phyllis as she and her friends hurried after Kim.

Chris grabbed my wrist and squeezed so hard it hurt. "Okay, see you then," she answered Phyllis in this chirpy little voice I'd never heard from her before.

"Yes! Yes! Yes!" Chris cried happily when the girls turned the corner. With each "yes" she thumped me excitedly on the arm.

"Cut it out," I grumbled.

"I did it," Chris said, smiling brightly. "We're having lunch with the coolest kids in our grade."

"Big whoopdy-do," I said sourly. "Maybe I don't want to eat lunch with them."

A look of horror crossed Chris's face. Then it passed. "You scared me for a minute. But I know you wouldn't let me down. We have to eat with them. We might never be asked again."

"She didn't invite me," I mentioned.

"Sure she did," said Chris. "You were standing there. You were part of the *you* in 'I'll tell you at lunch.'"

"Oh, okay," I agreed. "I guess it won't kill me."

"Not kill you?" Chris cried. "It might change your whole life!"

"Pul—lease!" I moaned. "Give me a break."

At lunchtime Chris dragged me over to the table where Kim and her friends sat. I felt completely out of place sitting down with them. Chris and I didn't belong there at all. Those kids knew it and I knew it. The only one who didn't seem to care was Chris.

If Chris felt awkward, she didn't show it. This startled me, because Chris had always been the shy one. I was the adventurous one. Now it seemed we had switched roles.

Kim barely noticed we were there. She sat talking to Gloria Chen, a tall, black-haired girl who was almost as pretty as Kim. Chris spent all her time talking to Phyllis and petite, blond Jessica. When Chris spoke, it was in a really fast, high-pitched, giggly voice. She totally forgot I was there, and left me feeling like a real jerk. No one spoke to me at all.

At one point, David Madison came over to the table and talked to Kim. I glanced at Chris. Her face went dead white, and then slowly started to turn pink. Very smooth, Chris, I thought sarcastically. You're certainly not giving yourself away. Not much. She might as well have painted a sign on her face saying, "I'm madly in love with David Madison."

I watched Kim as she spoke to David. She wasn't exactly delighted to see him. You know how a girl kind of perks up when a boy she likes comes around? Kim didn't do any of that around David. I couldn't tell if she was bored with him or if she was just *so* cool that it was hard to tell how she felt.

When the bell rang for the end of lunch, I

got rid of my tray without waiting for Chris. She was so busy talking to Phyllis that at first she didn't notice I'd left.

I was almost out the door before she realized I had gone. "Tracey, wait up!" she called, hurrying across the lunchroom. "Where are you going?"

"I figured you'd want to walk with Phyllis," I said. "Isn't she your new friend?"

"Come on, don't be like that," Chris pleaded.

"Christine, you didn't talk to me once during lunch!" I yelled. "Nobody did!"

"You didn't talk to anyone either," Chris shot back. "You just sat there like a lump."

"What was I supposed to talk about? I don't hang out at the mall. I don't know their little private jokes. Nobody asked my opinion about anything."

"Tracey, it wasn't a panel discussion. It was lunch. Everybody was jabbering away. Nobody was asking opinions. Don't be mad."

I really didn't want to be mad at Chris, but my feelings were hurt. I felt better now that she had come after me.

"Did you notice that David smiled at me?" Chris asked.

"No," I said flatly. "I noticed that you looked like you were about to pass out."

"I did not," Chris said with a scowl. "Did I? Did anyone notice? I didn't. You're just saying that."

"Maybe I was the only one who noticed," I said.

"Anyway, Phyllis invited us to go to the mall with them after school," Chris said.

"Us?" I asked.

Chris threw her arms up in the air. "Okay! She invited me. But I asked if you could come too, and she said, 'Sure.'"

This was getting to be too much! "I don't need an invitation from Phyllis Mann to go to the Greatdale Mall!" I shouted.

"Shhhh!" hissed Chris, looking around to make sure no one heard me. "It's not like that. You're too sensitive. She just said the kids were going to hang out there and did we—okay, I—want to come. And I just said you would be coming, too. Relax, would you?"

"You didn't say I was coming. You asked," I reminded her.

"It doesn't matter," Chris insisted. "Are you going to come with me, or not?"

"I don't know," I pouted. We walked together toward our lockers without talking. I had to think. After all, I had my pride. I had never tagged along after anyone else in my life, and I wasn't about to start now.

At that moment, I spied a sign on the wall that caught my attention: "Intramural Volleyball Tryouts." Chris and I loved to play volleyball. Lots of times in gym, Chris was captain of one team and I was captain of the other.

Midway had never had an intramural team before, though.

I ran to the sign and read it. The tryouts were in early November. "This will be fun," I said. "We'll definitely make the team."

"Definitely," agreed Chris, who had come up behind me. "And with you and me on the same team, we'll trounce all the other schools."

I smiled and felt good for the first time in weeks. The Chris I knew hadn't completely disappeared under all that make-up. She still loved volleyball and we were going to be on the team together. I could hardly wait.

We got our books from our lockers and headed toward our classrooms. I had science and Chris had honors English. She's a whiz at English. For the rest of the afternoon, we would be in different classes.

"See you later," she called to me as the bell rang. The stampede of kids rushing to class swept her along.

She was right. It was no big deal. It was just a day spent hanging around the mall. It might even be fun.

That's what I thought then, anyway.

As it turned out, it was a complete and total drag. Chris and I showed up at the movie theater. That's where the kids hang out. No one actually goes in to see the movie. They just stand around in front, or sit on the ledge near the fountain.

"Hi-hi!" Chris trilled when she spotted Phyllis, Gloria, and Jessica standing in front of the theater along with two boys and three girls from the ninth grade. When Phyllis saw Chris, she waved her hand excitedly.

"She's doing it!" Phyllis said, pointing to the other side of the fountain. There stood Kim and David, deep in conversation. Neither one of them looked too happy. "She's finally breaking up with him," Phyllis continued. "It's about time. She's been treating him really crummy for weeks."

"David is such a honey, too," said Jessica.

"Kim and David have just grown apart," said Gloria knowingly.

Chris looked as if she were in a state of shock. She actually staggered back a step. Her eyes were sort of glazed over. I poked her sharply in the side. "You okay?" I asked.

It was as if she barely heard me. "Uh-huh. I'm fine," she murmured.

We all stood and watched the scene. Kim's arms were folded with determination. She shook her head and turned her back on David. He looked angry, but he walked off in the opposite direction.

The kids paired off and went in two directions. The ninth graders went toward David. The eighth-grade girls headed for Kim. I felt a tug at my sleeve. "Aren't you coming?" Chris asked me.

"Where?" I asked. This was totally stupid as far as I was concerned. Why did everyone have to get involved in their business?

"I'm going with those other kids to make sure David is all right."

"You don't even know him or those kids," I reminded her.

"Traceeeeeeeeeeeeeeeee," Chris whined.

"You go. I'll wait for you here," I said. That was all it took. Chris was off and running after the "Help poor David" group.

After I read all the posters in front of the theater, I wandered around the mall for a while. When I returned to the theater, Chris *still* wasn't back. I stood staring up at the screen previewing the movies showing inside. I must have seen the same previews ten times.

I wasn't really mad at Chris, though. I suppose she figured this was her big chance with David.

She wasn't really wrong. In some ways you might say this *was* the beginning of her relationship with David.

And maybe it was also the point where our friendship began to fall apart. But I didn't realize that at the time.

CHAPTER

3

When Chris finally came back to the theater, she was wearing this phony look of sympathy and concern. I guess she didn't want all the kids to know how happy she was that Kim and David had finally broken up.

"He's totally heartbroken," she told me as we left the mall together. "I felt so bad for him."

"Get off it, Chris," I snapped. I was in a pretty rotten mood by this time. "You're happy and you know it."

"I'm not happy that David is so unhappy," she said seriously. "If you had talked to him, Tracey, you would understand. I think I said a few things that really made him feel better, though. He's such a sensitive boy. I knew that about him the minute I saw him."

I wanted to puke.

That evening, in my room, I took a good, hard look at myself in the mirror. What was the matter with me? Why wasn't I concerned about having a boyfriend? Why didn't I want to wear a ton of make-up?

Was I a case of stunted development?

Don't get me wrong. I like guys—as friends. And I think Johnny Dupré is completely gorgeous. I've seen all his movies. I've even dreamed about him a few times. I just can't picture dreaming about any of the guys I know personally. Maybe I don't know the right guys.

I gathered my thick hair up on top of my head and sucked in my cheeks. I did look slightly more glamorous. But I couldn't get a clip to keep my hair the way I wanted. It kept flopping over. And it isn't easy to speak with your cheeks sucked in.

I flopped down on the bed and wiggled my toes in the air. I would be thirteen in May. Chris was already thirteen. Was that the difference between us? Was thirteen some magical turning point? Next May would I, too, suddenly become obsessed with boys and make-up?

There was a knock on my door. Without

waiting for me to answer, my older sister, Connie, walked in. "Are you sick?" she asked, looking me over suspiciously.

"No. Why?" I said, sitting up on the bed.

"You went straight to your room when you came home," she explained. "Mom sent me up to check on you."

Connie had a boyfriend, Steve. She and Steve had been going together since they were fourteen. They were sixteen now. "Connie, when did you start liking boys?" I asked.

Connie grinned at me. "Are you in love?" she asked.

"No, I'm not in love," I snapped. "That's the problem. All the girls seem to be crazy about some guy or another. But not me. How come?"

Gazing into the mirror, Connie began to comb her long, dark hair. "I had a little crush on a boy in the sixth grade," she said. "But he wasn't interested in girls at all. Then I didn't like anyone else until I met Steve in high school. You haven't met the right boy yet, that's all."

"Why have the other girls in my class met the right boy?" I wanted to know.

Connie sat down at the edge of my bed. She began examining her hair, snapping off the split ends. She snapped about four ends before she answered me. "You know what a lot of girls do?" she began. "They pick a boy and say they like him, just because they want to be in on the boyfriend-girlfriend action. Boys do the same thing. It's not real, though."

"How do you know when it is real?" I asked.

"That's hard to say," Connie replied thoughtfully. "When you're really crazy about a boy, you can't think of anything else. At least at first. It's really annoying, in a way. I mean, you can do your homework and stuff like that. But the minute your mind isn't busy, that boy pops into it. The problem is, you can't tell until much later if it's true love, or just a super mondo crush."

"It sounds sort of disturbing," I commented.

"If the boy doesn't like you back, it's nause-ating," Connie said. "But it's so great if he does like you. Then you know that he's thinking about you all the time, too. It's the most wonderful feeling in the world." Connie got off the bed and headed for the door. "Don't worry, squirt. Your turn will come," she said as she left.

The next few weeks of school were strange for me. To my total amazement, Chris did get to know David Madison. A couple of times he even came to her locker to talk. When that happened, I just kept walking past Chris's locker. I didn't want to disturb her romantic chances, if there were any.

Kim started to date another ninth grader

named Paul Highland. When Chris got that news—from Patty Handleman, naturally—she acted as if she'd just won the lottery.

"There's nothing stopping me now!" she crowed happily.

"Why hasn't David asked you out yet?" I replied. "Did you ever consider the possibility that he just thinks of you as a really good friend?"

Chris wrinkled her brow. I knew she wouldn't want to hear what I had just said, but as her best friend, I had to point it out.

"That might have been true before, but it's going to change," she answered after a moment. "He's been mooning over Kim. I think he thought they'd get back together. Now that she's dating Paul, he's got to know it's completely over between them."

"Doesn't it bother you that he still has a thing for Kim?" I asked.

"A little," Chris admitted, tugging at her newly pierced ears. "But he'll get over it."

I sighed more loudly than I'd meant to. This David thing was dragging on longer than I had expected. I was tired of waiting for the old Chris to return. After all this time, I was still convinced she would change back once she stopped chasing David.

Then I remembered something that cheered me up. Volleyball tryouts were next week. But when I reminded Chris, she had a strange reaction. "I'm not sure I can be on the team," she told me.

I was stunned. And very upset. "Why not?" I cried.

Chris began chipping the purple polish from her nails. "I'm not doing so well in math. My mother says I should spend more time studying."

"Did she say specifically that you couldn't try out for volleyball?" I pressed.

"No," Chris answered sulkily.

"Then you have to try out with me. You said you would," I insisted, trying not to sound too upset. "Besides, you love volleyball!"

"I know, but I'm not sure I really want to be on the team," she said.

"Of course you do. You're a great player. You have to try out." I was sure volleyball was going to make us close again, the way we had been. I couldn't let her back out.

"Okay, okay! Calm down," said Chris. "I'll try out, already."

"Good," I said. It wasn't good, though. I wanted Chris to *want* this. "You'll see," I said. "Once we're on the team, it will be fun."

On the afternoon of volleyball tryouts, Chris was supposed to meet me at my locker. I waited and waited, but she didn't come. It was getting late, so I went around to her locker. She was standing there talking to David.

This time I didn't walk by. "Hurry up," I

interrupted their conversation. "We're going to be late."

"Late for what?" David asked.

I glared at Chris. She hadn't even told him.

"For the dentist," Chris lied. "I almost forgot. Tracey and I both have dentist appointments this afternoon."

"Ooohh." David winced. "Good luck."

"Thanks, we'll need it," said Chris, grabbing my arm and hurrying me down the hall.

"Why did you lie?" I asked as we headed toward the gym.

"What if I don't make the team?" she replied. "Then I'll have to admit it to him. I don't want him to think I'm a loser."

"If you don't make the team, then nobody will," I assured her.

When we got to the locker room, no one was there. "See, we're late!" I hissed at Chris. We quickly got into our shorts and joined the other girls in the gym.

"Okay! Here come the aces!" laughed a girl from our class named Peggy Sweeney as we hurried out onto the floor.

Ms. Russo, one of the gym teachers, separated us into two teams. There were more girls on each side than on a real team, but Ms. Russo said it didn't matter. She wanted to see how we played.

I smiled at Chris as she stood on the other side of the net. She smiled back tensely.

Peggy Sweeney made the first serve. Soon I was busy jumping and running for the ball. I made a couple of great saves, jumping in close to the net. In fact, I was so intent on playing well that it took me a while to realize that Chris hadn't returned a single ball.

She was sort of hopping around with her arms in the air, but she wasn't making any real effort. When my turn came to serve, I hit the ball as hard as I could. I wanted to send it all the way to the back line where Chris stood. I needed to see what she would do.

If my aim had been any better, the ball would have hit Chris on the head. It came right to her, but she ducked out of its path. "Look alive, Kirk!" Ms. Russo called to her as the ball rolled toward the gym door.

Even then, I was willing to believe that Chris was just having a bad day. When it was her turn to serve, though, I knew the truth. Chris sent the ball low and off to the side. It didn't even clear the net.

Chris has a great serve. She was purposely blowing this tryout!

I was furious. No, I was beyond furious. . . I was purple with rage. I was livid. I was . . . you get the idea. It was all I could do to finish the game.

Finally Ms. Russo blew her whistle to end the game. "The results will be posted tomorrow morning on the gym door," she announced. "Thank you, ladies."

Without waiting for Chris, I stormed into the locker room. In a few minutes she joined me. "Wow! This really wasn't my day," she said. "Did you see that serve? Good thing I didn't tell David about tryouts. I really don't think I—"

"Shut up, Chris," I said in a low, angry voice. "Just shut up, okay?"

"What's bugging you?" she asked. "It's not my fault if—"

There were a million angry things I wanted to tell her but they all got lumped together in my throat. For the first time in my entire life, I wanted to slap her.

Instead, tears welled up in my eyes. I wiped them away quickly. Crying was the last thing I felt like doing. "Go away, Chris," I said. "I don't feel like seeing your face right now."

Chris looked around anxiously, and I noticed a few girls were watching us. Now I was mortified as well as furious. Chris went to her locker and I continued to change. I didn't see her again until I was out in the hall. "Wait up," she called to me.

Suddenly, I found my words. "You creep," I said, whirling around to face her. "You deliberately washed out. I thought we could at least do *this* together, but you don't want to, do you? You never intended to make the team. That's why you didn't tell David about it. You were lying to me all along."

"I told you I didn't want to!" Chris shouted back. "But you kept insisting. Ever since first grade we've always done things your way. We watched horror videos because you like them. We played Monopoly all afternoon, because it was your favorite game. We even bought quarts of Double-Dutch Fudge Swirl ice cream because it's your favorite flavor."

"You love fudge swirl ice cream," was all I could think of to say.

"I like strawberry better," she said. "The point is, I've always done things that you want to do. I want to do things my way for a change. I'm not just a Tracey Loveridge clone. I'm me. I'm different from you."

I was stunned, to put it mildly. This was a whole new slant on things. But I was still mad.

"You should have been more honest about it," I said.

"I was honest, Tracey. You don't take no for an answer. And it's hard for me to say no to you. I'm not used to it."

"Are you saying I'm bossy?" I asked.

"Yes," Chris replied simply.

This was a lot to take in. I didn't realize I was bossy. I didn't want to be. It's just that when I want to do something, I'm usually convinced it's the right, or the smartest, or the most fun thing to do.

"What's right for you isn't always right for me," Chris added.

"Okay," I said. "I'll make you a promise. I will try as hard as I possibly can to be less bossy. All right?"

"All right," Chris agreed.

I meant it, too. I resolved then and there not to be so convinced that my way was the only way. I decided to really try to see things from Chris's point of view.

Looking back, this was probably one of the stupidest decisions I have ever made. Everything that went wrong after that was because of it.

CHAPTER 4

The next few months were kind of weird for me. In some ways, I really lost track of who I was. I was trying so hard not to be bossy or overbearing, that I became just the opposite.

I let Chris take the lead. This was a big turnaround for us. What Chris had said was true. It used to be me who did the leading. Now we started doing things her way.

When I look back, I realize something else. I was scared stiff of losing my best friend. I had always taken our friendship for granted. Everyone did. Chris and Tracey. Tracey and Chris. Always together.

Chris was like a part of me. Even though I

was the independent one (everyone said so), I couldn't picture myself without her. So I did what I thought needed to be done to keep our friendship together.

That meant I started hanging out at the Greatdale Mall, among other things. Chris now wanted to go there every day after school. By November it was obvious that Kim's crowd had accepted Chris. She wasn't one of the big shots like Kim or Gloria, or even Phyllis, but they didn't seem to mind her being there.

I never felt accepted though. I just sort of tagged along with Chris. I tried to like Chris's new friends, but all the girls talked about were the boys, with an occasional break for a fashion conversation. Since I didn't have much to say on either of these subjects, I listened a lot. I picked up some fashion tips, but otherwise it was pretty boring.

It wasn't boring to Chris, though. She spent all her energy on David Madison. Even though he and Kim had broken up, they both still hung around with the same people.

Chris got to know him pretty well. I hated the way she laughed at all his jokes. It wasn't that the jokes were bad, it was the way she laughed that annoyed me. She would laugh really loud, and even stagger back, holding her sides. His jokes weren't *that* funny.

She seemed so phony to me that I was sure

everyone else would think so, too. But nobody else noticed it. I even heard Phyllis say, "That Chris has such a great sense of humor. I never saw anyone laugh as much as she does." Apparently they were buying her whole routine. And why shouldn't they? They didn't know Chris the way I did.

I have to admit that Chris didn't desert me. In fact, she tried real hard to help me fit in with her new friends. "Tracey did the coolest thing yesterday," she would tell them. Or, she'd say, "You'll never believe what Tracey just told me. This will crack you up!" Unfortunately, the things I did and said never seemed cool or funny enough. Her new friends just smiled politely.

Most of the time, I wound up sitting on the ledge of the fountain, sipping a soda, while the other kids clowned around. It *looked* like I was with them, but I wasn't.

I didn't realize it then, but the only time I felt happy and like my old self was when I was playing volleyball. I made the team and—as you might have guessed—Chris didn't.

A girl on the team named Angie Mendez and I were getting to be pretty friendly. She was in one of the other eighth-grade homerooms and was new to Midway. She used to go to a private school.

I liked her a lot. She was very athletic, sturdy but not fat. Her dark hair fell down her back in a long, thick braid. She could really smash the volleyball over the net. We were the two best players on the team.

One day, right before Christmas vacation, Angie asked me over to her house. We were leaving the gym after volleyball practice.

"We just got a new pool table and I'm dying to try it out," she said as we walked into the hallway.

"I don't know how to play pool," I admitted.

"No problem. I'll teach you," she said.

"Okay, sure. I'll go call my mom and tell her," I said, heading for the pay phone in the lobby.

As I walked down the hall, a flood of emotions washed over me. I felt happy and terribly guilty all at once. I had told Chris I'd meet her at the mall that afternoon.

I was relieved at the thought of not going to the mall. There was this little bounce in my step that hadn't been there in a long time.

But, weaving itself around that feeling was another, uneasy, feeling. Chris would be expecting me at the mall. Would her feelings be hurt if I didn't show up? There was no way I could contact her. How would she feel if she called my house and my mother told her I had gone to Angie's?

I hadn't been to another girl's house since

third grade. Not alone, anyway. Chris and I visited other kids, but always together.

For a moment I stopped and thought about turning around. I would simply tell Angie I'd forgotten that I was supposed to meet Chris. I didn't go back, though. I kept right on walking to the phone and called my mother.

"Go, please, by all means," said my mother when I asked her. "I'm thrilled that you want to do something besides hang around that mall. Can Chris's mother pick you up?"

"Chris isn't going," I told her. "Just me. Angie lives over on Forsythia Lane. I can walk home."

There was a short silence on the other end. It was as if my mother couldn't grasp the idea that I was doing something without Chris.

That made two of us.

"Oh, okay," she said. "You two didn't have a fight, did you?"

My mother is always asking me questions that are—to be honest—none of her business. Usually I answer her. Sometimes I don't. For some reason, this question irritated me. "No, we didn't have a fight!" I snapped. "Aren't I allowed to do something without Chris?"

"Okay, okay. Sorry I asked," said my mother. "Are you sure you're all right?"

"I'm fine," I said.

It turned out that I was pretty good at playing pool and I picked it up very quickly. I hadn't expected it to be so much fun.

There was something else at Angie's that I hadn't expected—Roger. He was Angie's older brother. He was in the ninth grade at St. Luke's High School across town. Angie told me he was there on a track scholarship.

We were in the middle of a game when he came down to the finished basement. He looked a lot like Angie, dark and solidly built. But he was tall and his eyes were lighter than hers, more like a hazel color.

"Nice shot," he said as I sank a ball into a side pocket. "Who's winning?"

"We're just goofing around," Angie told him. "I'm teaching Tracey to play."

"Ready for a real game?" he asked me, taking a pool stick off the rack.

"Sure," I replied. "Why not?"

For some reason I was suddenly nervous. I stopped playing well. "You're holding the back end of the stick too high," Roger said. "Hold it like this." Gently, Roger lowered my elbow.

The weirdest thing happened. When he touched my elbow, my heart started pounding like crazy. It was so loud I was afraid he could hear it. But he didn't seem to notice.

I continued to play badly, but Angie and Roger didn't seem to mind. They teased me and teased each other. Eventually I relaxed and started hitting the ball again.

As I walked home from Forsythia Lane that evening, I had so much to think about. Was it finally happening? Was this love? A crush? Every time Roger stood next to me my heart would begin pounding again.

It was his eyes that got me. His eyes and the way he laughed. His laugh seemed to come from way down inside of him.

I decided to wait and see if the feeling wore off. Part of me was scared. I certainly didn't want to wind up like Chris, hanging around, thinking only about some boy. Besides, I couldn't believe that he would like me back. He probably thought of me as some little friend of his kid sister's—if he thought of me at all.

"Chris has called you seven times since five o'clock," said my mother when I walked in the door. "Please call her back. I'm tired of picking up the phone every ten minutes."

Talk about guilt! I felt terrible. Maybe she was worried about me. Or furious. "Did you tell her where I was?" I asked my mother.

"No, I just said you weren't home yet," my mother replied as she sat in the living room grading math papers. She's a teacher at Southside Elementary.

"Can I call her on your phone?" I asked. The rule in our house is kitchen-phone-only for my sister and me. But I knew I wanted privacy for this conversation.

"Keep it short," said my mother. I guess she realized this was important.

"Thanks," I said, climbing the stairs to her room. I didn't even get a chance to pick up the receiver before the phone rang. It was Chris.

"Before you say anything," I began, "let me explain. Something came up and I couldn't get to the mall. There was no way I could call you or I would—"

"It's okay," said Chris. "I figured your practice went late."

I had expected her to be furious with me for not meeting her. But instead she sounded happy.

"Wait till you hear this!" she bubbled into the phone. "I asked him. And he said yes! Can you believe it?"

"What are you talking about?" I asked.

"I asked David to go with me to the Date Dance, silly. Remember? And he said yes!"

I was speechless. Chris had mentioned that she wished she had the nerve to ask David to the dance. It was held in January right after Christmas vacation. It was the one dance during the year that you had to have a date for.

I never in a million years thought she'd go through with asking David. I figured she was just daydreaming out loud. "How did you get up the guts to do it?" I asked.

"It was perfect timing. He had just found out that Kim is going to the dance with Paul. I think David was hoping he might get back together with Kim in time for the dance. But now that she's going with Paul, he knows there's no hope. He was looking really down and gloomy. But he smiled when I asked him. It cheered him up a lot."

"It still doesn't bother you that he's so hung up on Kim?" I asked.

"He has to get over it sometime," she said. "A gorgeous hunk like him isn't about to stay unattached just waiting for Kim."

"Congratulations," I said. I was impressed. There was no denying that Chris had gotten further in her pursuit of David Madison than I had ever dreamed she would.

"Wait, wait. You haven't heard the second best part," she went on. "You are going to keel over when you hear this. I have a date for you, too!"

"What?" I yelped into the phone.

"David's best friend from camp is staying with David through the vacation. His school goes back a week later than we do. David asked me if I could fix him up with a date for the dance. Naturally, I thought of you."

"No way," I said immediately. "Forget it."

"Tracey, listen," Chris pressed. "This

friend is moving to Greatdale next year. If you guys like each other, he won't be far away for long. You'll have a boyfriend."

I pictured Roger's dreamy eyes when she said the word "boyfriend." "Ask someone else," I said firmly.

"Everyone else has a date already," she argued.

This surprised me. All the kids couldn't possibly be going to the dance. Then I realized what she meant. All the kids in Kim's crowd were already booked up. "What about Patty Handleman?" I suggested.

"Too fat," said Chris callously. The way she said it bugged me. Patty was on the plump side, but she wasn't really fat. It sounded snotty, like something Kim or Gloria might say.

"Then think of someone else," I protested.

"Tracey," said Chris, her voice low and serious. "You have to do this for me. I got the impression that if I can't get a friend for David's friend, then he won't go with me. I mean, he can't just leave his guest home, can he? If David went to the dance with someone else I couldn't stand it. I don't know what I would do."

When she put it that way, what choice did I have? "All right," I said, giving in. "I'll go. But what if he hates me?"

That's the kind of question you ask

because you want to be reassured that no one could possibly hate you. You expect a prompt answer from your best friend. She was supposed to say, "He'll be crazy about you."

Instead, I got silence.

Chris was actually seriously considering the possibility that he might hate me!

"No, no, I don't think he'll hate you," she said after a moment. "But just to be sure, maybe we should work on a few things."

"What things?" I cried indignantly.

"Don't worry," she said. "I'll be right over after supper."

Gently, I hung up the phone. A kind of sinking feeling came over me. What had I gotten myself into this time?

CHAPTER 5

$\mathcal{T}$he *few* things that Chris wanted to work on turned out to be me—my whole self. She made me her Christmas vacation project.

Why did I go along with it? At the time, I thought I was trying to be open-minded. Now I realize it was something more. Changing me was a project Chris and I could work on together. It had been a long time since we'd done anything together, just she and I, alone. It felt good to have her complete attention.

"How about becoming a blonde?" Chris suggested one afternoon as she eyed my hair thoughtfully. We were sitting in her bedroom working on Project Me.

"My parents would drop dead," I said. "I wouldn't be allowed out of the house until my real hair grew back." Fortunately, Chris knew this was true. It saved me from having to say that I was too chicken to bleach my hair blond. "I don't think I'd look good as a blond, anyway," I added.

Chris seemed to be of the opinion that everyone would look better with blond hair. "It's not supposed to look natural," she said. "It's supposed to look cool."

I wasn't so sure.

"I've got it!" she said, jumping off her bed excitedly. "Copper highlights and a perm. Yes! That's the look for you."

"I don't think you're supposed to color your hair and perm it at the same time," I pointed out. This was one of the few valuable bits of information I had picked up from our new *friends* at the mall.

"We'll start with the highlights, then," Chris decided. "How much money have you got? I have five dollars."

"Eight," I told her.

Chris considered this for a moment. "The hair place is out. It's too expensive. We'll have to do it ourselves."

"Do you know how?" I asked fearfully.

"It tells you on the box," Chris assured me. "I've been touching up my own roots. It's a cinch."

We walked down to the mall to buy the highlighting kit. When we got back to Chris's room, Chris tied a thin plastic cap over my head. There were holes in the cap. You were supposed to pull bits of hair through the holes with a thing that looked like a crocheting needle.

"Don't make it too red, okay?" I said as she began pulling hair through. "Ouch! And be careful with that thing! You're digging into my head."

"Sorry," she said. "You have so much hair it keeps tangling up under the cap."

"Well, just take a few strands through each hole," I warned nervously. "Don't pull big clumps of hair each time."

"Calm down," said Chris. "It's going to look great."

It took a long time to get the hair through the holes. "Chris," I asked, trying not to flinch each time the needle hit my scalp, "now that you know David, do you like him as much as you thought you would?"

"Sure I do," she said. "I like him so much I can hardly stand it."

"What is it you like about him?"

Chris stopped pulling hair. "I don't know," she said after a moment. "Everything, I guess."

What is it that makes us like some people and not like others? That was something I had been thinking about a lot. And it was what I went back to wondering about as I sat there being jabbed in the head with a blunt needle.

For example, why did I like Chris? I used to like her because we had fun together. The old Chris was a quiet person, but she always had this kind of devilish twinkle in her eyes. Not everyone saw it beneath those thick glasses, but I did. She would protest, then go along with whatever scheme I came up with.

"I can't wait for this dance," said Chris as she worked on my hair. "It is definitely going to be better than the dance we went to last year."

"Don't remind me." I laughed. That was the first dance we'd ever gone to. For most of it, Chris and I stood together, watching. Then this tough-looking eighth grader wanted to dance with me. He had a mean-looking face and I didn't like him. I said, "No thanks," as politely as I could.

Next thing I knew, a couple of his friends came up and said, "Do you think you're too good to dance with our friend?"

I didn't know what to say. As it turned out, I didn't have to say anything. Chris jumped in front of me. "You just get out of here," she yelled at them. "My friend will dance with whoever she wants. And, yes, she is too good to dance with your friend. Now get out of here before I call the chaperone!"

The boys glared at her, but they left.

"You really scared those guys." I chuckled, remembering how fierce she'd been. "Remember? There you were, this little person scaring these big guys. You were great."

Chris laughed. "I wasn't letting anyone pick on my best friend," she said.

At that moment, I found the courage to ask a hard question. "Are we still best friends?"

Chris stopped working on my hair. "How can you ask that?" She came around and stood in front of me. "I can't even picture us not being best friends," she said. "I would pulverize anyone who ever hurt you. I know you would do the same for me. Remember when we pricked our fingers and exchanged blood?"

"We were only seven," I reminded her.

"So what?" she cried. "That meant something. It did to me, anyway. We're blood sisters." Her eyes clouded with worry. "Don't you think we're still best friends?" she asked.

"Sure I do," I said, relieved by her answer. "I was just worried that since you have new friends and all . . . you know."

Chris went back to working on my hair. "Forget it," she said. "I like those kids, but you're my best friend. Do you think I would be here streaking your hair if I weren't?"

"I suppose not," I admitted. I was glad I had asked. In my heart, I knew Chris cared about me as much as I did about her. I just needed a little reassurance.

"Done!" Chris announced after a few more minutes.

I gazed into her bedroom mirror. I looked ridiculous. Hair was sticking up out of my head in all directions. "I would die if anyone else saw me like this," I said. "Didn't you pull an awful lot of hair through?"

"Stop worrying!" Chris said with a playful shove.

The next few steps were pretty easy. The hair glop went on, we waited, then showered it off. Getting the cap off took some tugging. Then I washed my hair and looked in Chris's bathroom mirror.

It was very—extremely—coppery.

"I adore it!" cried Chris. Kim and her friends always used the word "adore."

"I hate it!" I cried. My hair was the color of a shiny new penny with streaks of my old brown color mixed in.

"No you don't," Chris insisted. "It's just that you're not used to it yet." Putting her hands on my shoulders, she steered me out of the bathroom and back to her bedroom. "We'll dry it and set it with electric rollers. You'll adore it."

Chris did just that. When she was done, it looked like I had three times as much hair as usual. "Here's the finishing touch," announced

Chris, sweeping a handful of big loopy curls up to one side and holding it there with a fat hair clip.

"You look so great!" said Chris. "Of course, if you wear it that way you'll have to get your ears pierced."

"I don't know," I said, studying my image in the mirror. All my life I had thought I wanted red curly hair. But I wanted real red hair, not this strange, artificial color. "It's nice and all, but I'm not sure it's me," I said.

Chris threw up her hands in exasperation. "Who are *you*, Tracey?" she cried. "You're not even thirteen yet. How can you be so sure what's you and what isn't?"

She had a point.

How were you supposed to know? I just went along and did the things that felt the most natural. Chris, on the other hand, seemed to be creating herself day by day. She was forming a new identity, while I was most comfortable being the way I'd always been. Which of us was right?

There was one thing I did know. I might be the old me, but—thanks to Chris—I now had brand-new hair. I wondered if my mother would *adore* it as much as Chris did. Somehow I doubted it.

"I don't *believe* you're doing that," Chris complained as I used a bristly brush to smooth down all the curls. When I was done,

I gathered my hair back in a rubber band. It still looked coppery, but at least it wasn't so dramatic. I had a fighting chance of getting past my mother with my hair this way.

"I really appreciate all the work you did," I said as I pulled on my down jacket. "I'm sure you're right. I'll love it in a few days. Right now, though, all I can think about are my parents."

"Just stick to your guns," Chris advised. "I told my mother that it was my hair and I should be allowed to do what I wanted with it." Chris was forgetting that my parents were a lot more strict than hers. Her parents got divorced two years ago. Ever since then, they started going easier on Chris. I guess it was to make up for the divorce.

I wouldn't want my parents to get divorced, not for anything in the world. But I wouldn't mind it if they were a little less strict.

As I neared my house, I had to make a decision. Should I go in the front door or the back door? I wanted to pick the door where I was least likely to run into my mother. Of course, I couldn't avoid her forever. But right now I needed time to think. I had to come up with the best way to explain my hair to her.

I chose the back door, which led to the kitchen. Bad choice. Mom was right there preparing a salad for supper.

"Hi, Mom," I said, trying to sound natural.

Mom's eagle eyes always give me the once-over when I come in. It's just a split second where she makes sure everything is okay with me. I'm never sure what she's checking for—maybe broken bones or a sad expression. "Hi," she said, going back to her salad.

All right! I thought happily. She hadn't noticed my hair. If I kept it pulled back, maybe she'd never notice.

I was almost out of the kitchen when she took a second look. "Tracey Marie!" she said suddenly. As I'm sure you know, when a parent uses your full name you are just about always in trouble. "Come back here. What happened to your hair?"

I was wondering that myself, Mom. Isn't it odd?

Nothing happened to it. It's always been this color. You've just been too busy to notice.

These answers flashed through my head, but I was afraid they would only make matters worse. There was really no sense trying to get out of it. "Chris thought it might look nice with some highlights, so I let her try," I admitted.

I waited for an explosion. Instead, my mother folded her arms and leaned up against the counter. "Chris has been changing a lot lately, hasn't she?" she said.

That wasn't what I had expected her to say at all. I nodded.

"How do you feel about that?" she asked.

"I don't know," I said. "I mean, it's a free country. I guess she can change if she wants to."

My mother's eyes seemed to bore into me. "You know, you don't have to change just because she's changing."

"I know," I said.

When my mother cocks her head to one side, it usually means she doesn't believe something I've just told her. Her head was at a definite tilt right now. "I hope you know that," she said. "Because you're a sweet, lovely girl the way you are. You'll change in your own way, at your own pace. Trust me."

"Okay," I said.

She went back to slicing her tomato. "Stay away from your father until I have a minute to warn him about your hair. And that's it on the hair color. No more."

"I promise," I said. As I climbed the stairs to my room, I was completely shocked. I thought she was going to hit the roof. Her calmness amazed me.

Once I was in my room, I pulled my hair from its ponytail and studied it. Chris had been right—I was getting used to it. It actually looked kind of pretty in a strange sort of way.

If I hadn't been so worried about getting into trouble, I might have argued with my mother about Chris. How could we stay friends if I didn't change along with her? Wasn't it important to our friendship that I keep up with her changes? My mother didn't understand, I told myself.

Now that I think about all the things that happened after that, I've changed my mind. My mother understood more than I realized.

CHAPTER 6

By the night of the Date Dance in January, I looked exactly the way Chris wanted. She was extremely pleased. "Perfect," she announced as she slipped three bangle bracelets onto my wrist.

I had gone to her house to get ready for the dance, and I would be spending the night there. That way my parents would have nothing to say about my outfit. Chris had come up with this plan, and it had been good thinking. My mother would have had a fit if she saw how I looked.

My hair was back to the style Chris liked, curly and up on one side. She'd lent me one of her newest dresses. It was short, narrow, and hot pink.

"You're thinner than I am, Chris. It's too tight," I complained.

Chris studied me a moment, and then ran to her closet. She came back with a long, lightweight yellow jacket. "Put this on," she suggested. Then she pushed up the sleeves and fastened some rhinestone pins to the pockets. "Totally cool," she said, turning me toward her bedroom mirror.

Earlier, Chris had done my make-up. My eyes were lined and shadowed. I was wearing a shade of her lipstick that matched the dress exactly.

"I look like a kid playing dress-up," I said to Chris. That's how I felt, too.

Chris put her arm around my shoulder. "Relax. We both look great," she said.

By now, I was used to the way Chris looked. Tonight she wore a short black skirt and a furry, electric-blue sweater. She'd gelled her hair up at the sides and left it feathery at her neck. She wore long, sparkly earrings.

Mrs. Kirk drove us to the dance. My stomach ached all the way there. I was worried about everything. What would David's friend be like? Would he like me?

I was glad Angie Mendez wasn't going to the dance. I couldn't have faced her looking the way I did. She would have laughed and said I looked silly. During vacation, I had gone to her house three more times. I really liked her. I wasn't going just to see Roger, but I couldn't help looking for him.

He was only there one of the three times that I went. When I saw him come in with two of his friends, I felt the same heart-fluttery way I'd felt the first time I'd met him. He smiled at me and said, "Hi, Trace."

The way he said "Trace" instead of Tracey was very encouraging. Only people who like you fool around with your name.

Mrs. Kirk pulled up to the back door of the school. The parking lot was crowded with kids being dropped off.

"There they are!" Chris cried excitedly as we walked toward the school. By the door stood David and his friend. She squeezed my arm. "Isn't he gorgeous?"

I knew that she had to be talking about David. Gorgeous was not a word that anyone in their right mind would have used to describe my date. He was short, skinny, and shifted constantly from one foot to the other. He wore a red, purple, yellow, and green jungle-print jacket with really baggy black pants. "Hey, looking foxy," was the brilliant way Vinnie greeted me. Things went downhill from there.

Almost immediately, Chris and David

began dancing. Vinnie and I were left alone to chat.

I quickly discovered that Vinnie and I had only one thing in common: height. If he had been short but nice, I wouldn't have cared. I'm not a giant myself. He wasn't nice, though.

Although I was not impressed with Vinnie's looks or personality, Vinnie was—impressed with himself, that is. He tugged at the sleeves of his jungle-print blazer and informed me, "I can't wait to start Midway next fall. My love life over at Eastbrook was getting too complicated. A new school means a new start. Fresh chick pool to pick from."

"I know what you mean," I replied snidely.

Vinnie didn't pick up on my sarcasm. He seemed to think I was serious. "Hey, if you have a main man here that I should know about, tell me now. I don't need any problems with any huge football types." As he spoke, he gazed nervously around the room as if waiting for some gigantic former boyfriend of mine to step out of the crowd.

"It's nothing like that," I assured him.

A breath of relief whooshed from his lips. "Good, because I am very tough and I wouldn't want to have to hurt the guy," he said.

This breathtaking conversation came to a brief halt when Vinnie spotted Carolyn Liberti, a quiet but very pretty girl from my homeroom. "Fox-arooni," he muttered under his breath as she passed by on her way to the refreshment table.

Then he spotted Helena Walsh. I had never considered Helena that great-looking, just sort of average. But Vinnie thought otherwise. "Mmmmmmmm-ummmm," he murmured in appreciation.

I was beginning to find this extremely annoying. We had a long night ahead of us, though, and I wanted to make the best of it. "Want to dance?" I asked.

"You bet," said Vinnie, grabbing my hand and heading out to the dance floor.

The music was loud and fast. But Vinnie was faster. He seemed to be dancing to a beat all his own as he threw himself around. His head jerked back while his shoulders came forward. He hopped and spun and then did a split right on the floor. While he was down there, he kicked up his legs and spun on his bottom.

As you can imagine, the kids began to notice him. I didn't know what to do, so I just kept bopping around to the music. It probably looked like I was out there dancing by myself. Vinnie made no effort to include me in his dance. This was a one-man show.

The song seemed to go on forever. Finally

it ended. Proud of himself, Vinnie pushed his hair back with two hands and smiled at me. I managed to return a weak smile.

In a second, the next song came on and Vinnie was at it again. He took his jacket off and tied it around his waist. For this number, he seemed to feel he needed a partner. He grabbed my wrists and began yanking me in, then tossing me away. I felt like a yo-yo. All the while he kept bobbing his head up and down as if it were on a spring.

As I was yanked back and forth, I looked out at the kids dancing nearby. My heart leaped into my throat. There was Roger! He was dancing with some girl from the ninth grade, whom I'd seen around but didn't know.

It was horrible. He was watching Vinnie and me, and there was laughter in his hazel eyes. I wanted to die.

As if things weren't bad enough, Vinnie picked that moment to send me twirling out into the crowd. Our sweaty hands slipped apart and I kept right on going until I crashed into a couple who were dancing near Roger.

"Excuse me. I'm so sorry," I muttered, completely mortified.

"No problem," said the boy I had run into. "I didn't need those toes, anyway."

Of course, Roger saw what happened. He

stopped dancing for a moment. "Are you okay?" he asked.

"Yeah, sure," I replied, tugging down my short skirt.

He smiled and nodded over toward Vinnie. "Better get back before your date realizes you're gone," he teased.

Sure enough, Vinnie wasn't even aware that I wasn't dancing with him. He had gone into another set of solo spins.

All I could think to do was wait for the music to end. When it did, Vinnie was panting and sweaty, but extremely pleased with himself. He seemed to be waiting for a compliment. "How's it feel to dance with a wild man?" he asked, when I failed to deliver.

"Lonely," I replied. "And kind of hazardous to my health."

This was not the response Vinnie had expected, and it ticked him off. "That's not my fault. Loosen up," he snapped. "David warned me you were kind of stiff, but I told him the Vin-man could warm up any chick."

Now *I* was ticked off. "I'm not *any* chick," I snarled. "In fact, I'm not a chick at all. Do you see any yellow feathers on me?"

Raising both hands, Vinnie backed away. "Hey, save the bad attitude, huh?"

"Sorry," I said. "But so far this evening you've referred to me as a fox, then a chick. What other animals do I remind you of?"

"How about one that says, 'bow-wow'?" Vinnie shot back.

I guess I set myself up for that one. Still, it stung like a slap. Logically, I shouldn't have cared what he said. He was a geek and a creep. Even so, it hurt to be called a dog— even by a jerk.

I felt the warning tingle of tears around my eyes. "Why don't we just call this a disaster and go our own ways?" I suggested, determined not to cry.

"Suits me fine, babe," agreed Vinnie.

Without another word, I stormed away from him. The teary feeling in my face faded. It was replaced by a kind of sickening lump in the pit of my stomach. It was a lump of disappointment. Even though Chris had forced me into this evening, the truth was that I had been kind of excited about it. I had pictured Vinnie to be a great guy who would be super-attracted to me. I had dreamed we'd have a great time, and he'd ask me out again.

This fantasy made me feel a little disloyal to Roger. But, I told myself realistically, Roger wasn't exactly beating the door down to date me. To him I was just a goofy little friend of his sister's.

I settled down on one of a group of folding chairs that had been set up in a corner. I watched Roger dance with his date. How handsome he looked in his dark blue sports jacket! He was a good dancer, too. Unlike Vinnie, he moved *with* the music, not in spite of it.

The girl he was with was really pretty in a very natural way. She had wavy dark hair and a great figure. I'd never had the nerve to ask Angie if Roger had a girlfriend. Now I didn't have to.

So that was the kind of girl he liked. Compared with his date, I looked like I was dressed for a costume party.

The lump of disappointment got even heavier as I watched them together. They laughed and looked completely relaxed. It was clear that they really liked one another a lot.

It's funny how many things you see when you just sit and observe—things you might not notice, otherwise.

One thing I noticed was that Kim and her new boyfriend didn't seem to be having a great time. On the surface it might have looked like they were having fun, but there was a kind of faraway gaze in Kim's eyes.

I caught her looking at David and Chris a couple of times. I suppose that was natural enough, but there was something in her expression that worried me. She seemed upset when she looked at them. If she didn't care about David anymore, why should it bother her that he was with Chris?

The really worrisome part was that I

noticed David looking back at her. They were just quick peeks, but he was definitely looking. One time, their eyes met and they both turned away.

Chris didn't notice any of this. She was in heaven. Her hand never let go of David's. At every slow dance she nuzzled her head into his shoulder like a contented kitten.

Although David was secretly eyeballing Kim, he was pretty attentive to Chris. When they danced he held her tight. He made it very clear that he was there with her.

Occasionally I would catch a glimpse of Vinnie spinning around the dance floor like a demented top. Once he actually danced with Carolyn Liberti, much to my surprise.

All this interested me in a depressing kind of way for about forty minutes. Then I began to feel that I must look like a real sad sack sitting there all alone. Some of the girls and guys from my class waved as they passed. A few girls stopped by briefly, but they were all with dates, so they didn't stay around long.

Gradually, I began getting more and more annoyed at Chris. She was so wrapped up in David that she didn't even bother to come see how I was doing.

Someone *did* notice, though. My heart began pounding as Roger approached me. If things had been different, I would have been ecstatic. As it was, I felt self-conscious about my outfit and somewhere between pitiful and ridiculous. My self-confidence was not at its all-time high.

"You unloaded the human cannonball, huh," he said lightly as he sat beside me.

I nodded, smiling glumly. "Yeah, he seems all busted up about it, too," I joked as we watched Vinnie drag another dance victim onto the floor with him.

"He wasn't your type," Roger observed kindly. "You look kind of different yourself tonight."

I folded my arms and tucked my legs under the chair. More than anything in the world, I wanted to disappear. "I was trying out a new look," I said.

"I liked your old look better," he replied.

That was honest enough. He didn't say it in a mean way, either. That was just how he felt.

I shrugged. "I guess you don't know until you try."

"Guess not," he said, getting up. "I'd better get back to Sue Ellen before she gets mad at me."

Sue Ellen. I suddenly hated that name.

"So long," I said.

"Bye," he said with a wave as he headed off across the dance floor. I wanted to scream, kick my feet, have a tantrum. He was so nice. But he thought I looked dumb, and he had a girlfriend. So that was that.

Finally, I couldn't take it anymore. I noticed Chris standing by herself, so I grabbed the opportunity to talk to her alone. "What happened to Vinnie?" she asked me.

"He was spinning so hard he broke loose of Earth's orbit," I answered angrily. "He may be spinning past Venus now for all I know!"

"I guess you're not having a very good time, are you?" she said.

"Can't you tell that I'm having the greatest time of my life?" I snapped. "If I were having any more fun I might just keel over and faint."

"Okay, don't get snotty with me," she said defensively. "I suppose this means you want to leave?"

"Would you mind?" I asked, relieved.

"David went to the boys' room," she said. "Let me go out to the hall and find him. Then I'll call my mother."

"Thanks," I said. "I'll wait here."

Wait is exactly what I did—for almost twenty minutes. Then I headed out of the cafeteria and down the hall to find Chris.

There was no sign of her. I saw Patty Handleman standing in the hallway talking to her date—a tall, heavyset guy who must have been from another school. "Have you seen Chris?" I asked.

Patty thought a moment. "Yeah. I saw her leave with David about ten minutes ago."

"What . . ." I stammered. "Are you sure? I thought we weren't allowed to go in and out of the building."

"I think they slipped out when Mr. Caffrey wasn't looking," said Patty. "If I see her, should I tell her you're looking for her?"

"If you see her, tell her to drop dead!" I cried, furious. Wiping my lipstick on the back of my hand, I stomped to the lobby to call my parents to come get me. I had made up my mind. I was never speaking to Christine Kirk again!

CHAPTER

All day Sunday, Chris called and called. I wouldn't talk to her, though. I felt hurt and humiliated. How could my best friend treat me so thoughtlessly?

"Chris says to tell you she intended to come back inside to get you," said my mother after taking Chris's zillionth call.

"Yeah, when she was good and ready to come in," I commented sourly. I was lying on the living room floor watching a nature special on TV. Giant eagles swooped in the sky, looking majestic and free. That's all I can tell you about the show, because I wasn't really watching it. I was too busy thinking about how angry I was at Chris.

"She says she's not calling back again," added my mother.

"Good," I snapped.

"Maybe you should talk to her," my mother suggested.

"No way," I replied firmly. I was the one who had done all the bending and giving in. *I* had changed my looks. *I* had gone to the mall day after dreary day. *I* had let myself be spun around by Vinnie, the crazed Romeo.

Well, it was done. Finished. I wasn't bending anymore. From now on I was going back to being me, Tracey Loveridge, plain and simple.

"The past is dead," I told my mother. "I'm getting on with my life."

"I see," she said. I didn't like the hint of amusement on her face. She obviously didn't understand that this was a big turning point for me.

Up until now my life had been woven in with Chris's life. We were like a striped fabric. Maybe I was the red stripe and she was the blue, but we had belonged together. Now we no longer did.

I was a red stripe wandering around with nowhere to go.

This might have made me feel sad, but I was too angry. Sad was the last thing I wanted to be right now. I went into the kitchen and called Angie Mendez. "Are you doing anything today?" I asked.

"Not really," she said. "Want to play some pool?"

"I'll be there in half an hour," I told her. I was glad Angie was free. All I wanted to do right now was forget all about Christine Kirk. I couldn't exactly accomplish that by moping around my living room being angry at her.

I washed my face and put my hair back in a ponytail. It felt good not to have to gel and curl it. I wondered if Roger had told Angie about seeing me at the dance.

When I got to Angie's, she and I helped ourselves to some milk and cookies and then went down to the basement to play pool. "Roger said you didn't have such a good time at the dance," said Angie as she placed the pool balls into the triangle on the table.

From the heat on my cheeks, I knew I was blushing. "No, it was kind of a disaster," I admitted.

Angie giggled. "He said your date was a wild character. Who was he?"

Rolling my eyes, I went ahead and told Angie the whole story of how Chris had pressured me into going on this date. "That certainly explains it," said Angie, leaning on her pool stick.

"Explains what?" I asked.

"It explains the way you looked. Roger said he didn't even recognize you at first. I should have known Chris Kirk was behind it. I can't understand how the two of you can be friends. You're nothing alike. Why do you let her push you around?"

"She doesn't," I answered defensively. I never thought of myself as someone who got pushed around, especially not by Chris.

"Sure she does," insisted Angie as she picked up the white cue ball and shot it into the colorful formation of balls on the table. "Everyone says so."

"Who is everyone?" I asked.

"I don't know. Kids."

This was horrible. I've never cared a whole lot about what other people thought of me. Maybe that was because most of the time, other people thought well of me. It was embarrassing to think that kids in school saw me as Chris's wimpy friend. How had I let things get so out of hand?

At that moment, Roger came down the stairs. I tucked a stray strand of hair behind my ear and straightened my shirt. I knew he had a girlfriend, but I couldn't help myself. I wanted him to see that I was back to my regular look.

"Hi," he said with that smile that made my knees quiver. He looked me up and down quickly. I could tell he was noticing that I was my old self again. He didn't comment, though.

"Sue Ellen called this morning," Angie told

him. "She said to thank you again for taking her last night."

Roger was digging for something in a chest full of sports equipment. "I wish she would stop thanking me," he said absently as he rummaged. "It was no big deal."

No big deal? That was an odd thing to say about taking your girlfriend to a dance. "Why is Sue Ellen thanking Roger for taking her to the dance?" I asked after Roger left.

"Oh, this guy she was going with dumped her right before the dance. She was all heartbroken and disappointed about the dance, so she asked Roger to take her."

"You mean he's not her regular boyfriend?"

Angie snorted with laughter. "Sue Ellen is our cousin."

"Cousin!" I cried. "Oh, wow! That's great!"

Angie's dark eyes sparkled. "I don't believe it," she said. "You have a crush on Roger."

I didn't know why, but I felt as though I'd just been caught committing some terrible crime. "Not really," I lied, flustered.

"You do, too. You're blushing," Angie pointed out. There was no denying it. My cheeks were red-hot.

"Okay, so I think he's pretty cute," I admitted. "But that's not why I come over here to see you or anything." I wanted to make sure Angie understood that. It would have been terrible if she thought I was using her to get to Roger.

"Are you sure?" she asked, sounding hurt.

"Of course," I said. "I called you this morning even though I thought Roger was already taken."

"Okay, I believe you," she said, brightening. "I can't believe you thought Sue Ellen was his girlfriend."

"They seemed so relaxed together," I said, recalling the easy way they had joked with one another.

"They should be," Angie scoffed, sending a pool ball right into a side pocket. "We all practically grew up together. Sue Ellen lives two houses down." Angie stepped back and squinted at me. "I could kind of see you with Roger. His old girlfriend looked a little like you. They had to break up because she moved. He was totally bummed for a long time."

"Does he have a girlfriend now?" I dared to ask.

"Nope," said Angie. She leaned into another shot, her long braid sweeping the table. "I have to warn you, Roger can be a real pain sometimes. When a football or basketball game is on, he doesn't care what I want to watch. And when he takes a shower, forget it. He doesn't come out for about a thousand years. It's extremely annoying."

"My mother says I take too long in the shower, too," I replied.

"Then you're two of a kind," said Angie. "I can't wait to tell him you like him."

My heart leaped into my throat. "No, don't do that!" I said urgently.

"How else will he know you like him?" Angie argued.

That was a good question. "But I'll just die if you tell him," I wailed. "It will be so embarrassing. He'll think I'm chasing after him. I know he doesn't like me back."

"I wouldn't be so sure," said Angie, neatly sinking another ball into the pocket. "He was talking about you a lot when he got home from the dance last night. He said he felt really sorry for you."

"Great," I moaned dismally. "Pity isn't the emotion I was hoping for."

Angie shrugged. "I don't think it was pity. Not exactly." This time her shot missed and hit the other balls with a clank. "Do you want me to tell him or not?"

"No," I decided. "Don't tell him."

"Are you positive?" Angie pressed.

I picked up my pool stick and aimed at a red ball. My stick connected at a funny angle and the ball bounced across the table and then came to a dead stop. Not exactly my most impressive move. "Positive," I said uncertainly.

As I walked home from Angie's that afternoon, my head ached. My thoughts were all jumbled together. I tried to sort them out.

Question number one was, did I have a right to be mad at Chris? The answer was yes, definitely. The more difficult question was, did I really, truly want to stay mad at her?

My mother always says to listen to your heart, so I tried to do that now. And my heart told me that I *did* want to stay mad at her. Besides, I didn't enjoy being with her anymore.

Yes, I had liked the time we spent together over vacation as we "fixed" my image. But I didn't like her new friends, and those friends were now part of her life. They had become more important to her than I was.

I was still angry at Chris and I intended to stay that way.

The next question was, how did I feel about Roger? All I knew for sure was that I loved to look at him. Every move he made seemed so perfect, so graceful. He was so warm and nice. There didn't seem to be a jerky bone in his body. Angie only found him annoying because she was his sister. Connie and I were always annoyed with each other over some stupid little thing. It was never serious.

Oh, if only he would like me! My imagination began to go crazy. I imagined running into him as I walked down the street. That would be the best way. We would talk and everything would be so easy. Then he would fold me in his arms and kiss me.

I couldn't believe I was thinking these things! It wasn't like me at all. Even when I thought about Johnny Dupré, I imagined we were on a great adventure together, battling mutant termites or freeing the planet from an alien invasion.

It was all too strange. Yet I couldn't get the thought out of my mind. I kept seeing that romantic image of Roger kissing me.

This picture of Roger and me wasn't like any fantasy I'd ever had about Johnny Dupré. Roger wasn't saving me from anything that had mutated. My daydreaming about Roger was simple, warm—and realistic.

Then it struck me. This was the feeling Connie had been telling me about. I was in love. Or I had a mondo crush.

A twinge of guilt came over me. Was this how Chris felt about David? Probably. It was a pretty powerful feeling, and it didn't make it easy to think straight. I suddenly had a new insight into how Chris must be feeling.

I squashed that thought right away. I didn't want to make any excuses for Chris.

No sooner was I inside my house than I was greeted by my father wearing a very aggravated expression. He ran his hand across the bald spot on top of his head. With him, that's always a bad sign. And, even though he's tall, when he's angry he manages to look even taller.

"Tracey," he said in a voice that was loaded with forced self-control. "Chris has been calling this house nonstop since you left."

"She said she wasn't going to call anymore," I told him.

"Well, I guess she didn't mean it," he said irritably. "Your mother asked you to talk to Chris earlier today. *I* am now asking you. No, I am ordering you, to speak to her the next time she calls. Your mother has to get papers graded for tomorrow. And I have been trying—in vain—to take a nap. We are both going to go berserk if that phone rings one more time."

At the end of his last sentence, his voice quivered a little. I knew he meant business.

"Okay, okay, I—" I was cut off by the sound of the phone.

My father's eyes kind of bulged. "Stay calm," I said, racing into the kitchen. "I'll get it."

Quickly, I snatched up the receiver. "You're driving the whole house crazy," I barked into the phone. "I have nothing to say to you, so what do you want?"

For a moment there was silence on the other end. Then, "Tracey, is that you?" someone asked.

It was Roger.

CHAPTER

$\mathbb{I}$ couldn't believe my ears! It was really Roger.

After I apologized for the way I picked up the phone, he asked if I wanted to go to an indoor fair at his school the following Saturday. "It sounds goofy but it's really pretty fun. There's always good stuff to eat," he said. "A bunch of my friends are going, too."

"It sounds great," I answered, trying to keep my voice from quivering with excitement. "What time?"

"I'll come to your house around twelve, if that's okay."

"Sure. It sounds good," I replied. I searched desperately for something witty or clever to say. Absolutely nothing came to me. "Okay then," I said like a dimwit.

"Okay," he answered. At least he wasn't doing much better than I was.

"Is Angie around?" I asked.

"Yeah, just a second, I'll get her." He sounded relieved to get off the phone. I suppose it's always awkward asking someone out for the first time. In a minute Angie was on the line.

"You told him, didn't you? I know you did," I accused her.

For a moment there was silence. "All right, so I told him," she whispered. "He says he thinks you're cute. He didn't exactly waste time doing something about it, did he?"

"I guess not," I admitted.

"So? What are you complaining about? You like him. He likes you. I just brought it out into the open. You should thank me."

"Thanks," I said. She was right. It was just that I was feeling self-conscious. "Does he know that I didn't tell you to tell him?"

"I told him you *swore* me to secrecy." She laughed. "Really, I did."

"Okay," I said, feeling better. "I'll see you tomorrow."

As I hung up, I realized my heart was pounding like crazy. Roger had called me! I was going on my very first date. It was too good to be true.

My first impulse was to dial Chris's number. For years now I'd always called her right away when something great—or something awful—happened. But now I couldn't call her. We weren't friends anymore.

For a moment, I considered forgetting our fight and calling her. I couldn't, though. I was just too angry at her.

Maybe I would mention it the next time Chris called. But Chris didn't call again. She must have decided to corner me at school.

All the next week Chris tried to talk to me in person. It was pretty easy to avoid her. I bolted from my locker as soon as I got my books. At lunchtime, I wolfed down my sandwich and went to the gym. Angie and I and some of our friends from the volleyball team had gotten permission to practice.

Of course, Chris didn't spend all her time trying to track me down. She spent a lot of it with *her* new friends. Especially with David. You would have thought someone had glued their hands together.

Their group had splintered into two factions. There was the original group with Kim at its center, and then there was a group with David and Chris at its center. That group was made up mostly of ninth graders. It was generally considered to be even cooler than Kim's group. I had to hand it to Chris—she was now one of the most popular kids in the school.

At the end of the week I found a note from Chris stuck in my locker.

Dear Tracey,

First off, let me say that I wasn't going to leave you stranded at the dance. It was just that David wanted to talk to me about something private so he asked if I would step outside for a minute. Then he started kissing me and it was really wonderful. So I kind of lost track of time. It's not easy to tell a boy you're nuts about to stop kissing you. You should have given me a break and waited. Besides, we had to wait for the right moment to sneak back in, since we weren't supposed to have gone outside to begin with.

Maybe if you ever like a boy the way I like David you will understand. I think the way you're avoiding me is very mean. I can't believe you are willing to end our best-friendship over a misunderstanding. I'll forgive you if you forgive me.

Love,
Chris

He kissed her! I don't know why that was so surprising. I should have expected it. But still, it was her first kiss. I wanted to hear all about it.

The problem was that I couldn't stop remembering how dumb and left out I had felt standing there waiting and waiting for her to return.

I folded the letter and put it in my pocket. I had to think about it. After all, I could almost understand how being kissed for the first time might make you lose track of time. But on the other hand, she could have gotten herself together enough to remember me waiting inside. Of course, I didn't know for sure. I had never been kissed before, either.

On Saturday afternoon the doorbell rang at exactly twelve. "Why is everyone hanging around?" I cried as I ran to let Roger in. My mother, father, and Connie were all sitting in the living room.

"Excuse us, we just happen to live here," said Connie, pretending to watch TV.

"How dumb do I look, Connie?" I snapped back. My family *never* sits together in the living room on a Saturday afternoon. Obviously, they were there to inspect Roger.

"Shouldn't you open the door?" asked my mother. She had a newspaper open in front of her. My mother *always* reads the paper *after* supper.

My father wasn't even pretending. He just sat there, with his eyes glued to the door. "Maybe I should answer the door," he said, getting up.

"No! I'll get it," I said quickly. I opened the door just as Roger lifted his hand to ring again.

"Hi," he said, smiling his great smile. "I was afraid I had the wrong house."

"No, this is the right house," I replied. "Come on in."

My father was on his feet in an instant. He was friendly, but he was doing whatever it is he does to make himself look really tall. "Hello, Roger," he said, shaking hands. "It's nice to meet you. Tracey tells me that this fair ends before dark."

"That's true, sir," said Roger. Right away, I could see my father warm up. "We should be home by five," Roger added.

"Five-thirty will be fine," said my mother as though she were bestowing some great gift upon us.

"Give the kids a break!" Connie piped up. "Why don't you go all out and let them stay out until six?"

"As I said, five-thirty will be fine," said my mother.

"In case you haven't guessed, these are my

mother and sister," I told Roger as I pulled on my jacket.

"I guessed. Hi," said Roger.

"You kids have fun," my father said. "But, remember, Roger, this is my little girl."

"Dad!" I wailed. This was too embarrassing!

"Let them go, would you?" cried Connie. I owed her one for that.

Finally we made it out of the house. "Sorry about my family," I said as we headed down the block. It was a freezing cold day. My words formed small clouds of smoke in front of my mouth.

"No problem," he said. "I think all fathers are like that when it comes to their daughters."

"I guess," I replied.

It wasn't far to St. Luke's. The school looked very different from Midway Junior High. Midway is modern with clean, sharp lines. St. Luke's was tall and square with an old-fashioned stone front. Saints carved in stone looked down at us as we went through the front door. "This is a pretty school," I said sincerely.

Roger laughed lightly. "Do you think so? It just looks like St. Luke's to me. It's a good school, though. I like it here."

We walked into the gym. It was set up with all sorts of booths. There were games with prizes and a spin-art T-shirt booth where you could design your own shirt. There was a man analyzing handwriting with a computer and all sorts of crafts for sale. As Roger had said, there was a whole bank of tables set up with food—pizzas, hot sausage, hamburgers, and lots of baked stuff.

Two girls and two boys met up with us. Alice and Melanie were both pretty. Alice had short blond hair and Melanie was tall with long brown hair. Roger's friends Alec and Stewart were both on the track team with him. They were cute, but not as good-looking as Roger.

I couldn't tell if they were couples or just friends. It didn't seem to matter. They were very friendly to me. All of them were in the ninth grade.

Things were going great. As Roger and I started to go from booth to booth, the shyness we both felt fell away. In a short while we were laughing and kidding around.

Then I spotted Chris.

She was standing all the way at the other end of the gym with David and a bunch of their friends. "What's the matter?" asked Roger. "What are you looking at?"

"Those kids," I said, pointing across the gym. "They don't go to St. Luke's. What are they doing here?"

Roger looked in Chris's direction. "That kid

100

goes here," he said, pointing at a tall, thin boy with sandy-blond hair. "But he hangs out over at Midway. He's a real idiot, always making trouble."

Taking another look, I realized that I had seen him with David once or twice.

"What are you guys looking at?" asked Alice. "Oh, Todd Munson is here with those Midway jerks again."

"Watch what you say," said Roger. "Tracey goes to Midway. So does my sister."

"I didn't mean everyone from Midway was a jerk, but those kids are," Alice said. "I hope Stewart doesn't see him," she added. "Todd and Stewart almost had a fist fight at the basketball game last week. They've been enemies ever since Todd beat Stewart up in the fifth grade."

"Well, they're not bothering us, so let's forget about them," Roger said, steering me over to the pizza booth.

Unfortunately, Chris *was* bothering me. I couldn't stop myself from looking over at her. And when she finally saw me, she kept sneaking peeks, too.

I suppose eventually it was bound to happen. The two groups met at the baked goods table. I studied the brownies as though my life depended on picking the right one.

That's why I wasn't really paying attention to what happened next. Roger was horsing around with Stewart. They were tossing around a wrapped brownie that Roger had just bought. Then Stewart stumbled and fell into Todd Munson.

"Watch it, pinhead!" Todd growled.

"Who are you calling a pinhead, you slime bucket?" Stewart shot back.

After that, everything flew very quickly out of control. Todd hit Stewart. Stewart hit him back, sending him flying into David. David then jumped on top of Stewart. While Roger was pulling David off Stewart, Todd hit Roger right in the mouth. This infuriated Alec, who jumped into the fight. And then more guys from the other side joined in.

I was horrified. I glanced over at Chris to see how she was taking all this. For a moment I considered suggesting that she and I both just get the heck out of there. But when I looked at her, I was stunned. She was really into the fight. "Get him, David!" she was yelling. "Get him!"

And she was saying this as David was punching Roger!

In the next second, two priests were pulling the boys apart. Everyone spoke at once. "He started it!" "Did not!" "You're a jerk!" "Go back to Midway!" "St. Luke's loser!"

Not surprisingly, the priests threw all of us out. Well, the boys, anyway. But the girls left, too. Once we were all outside there were more nasty words, but no more punches were thrown. I saw Chris glaring over at our group. She seemed so far away, like a stranger.

The Midway kids finally headed off. We began walking in the opposite direction. "I'm going to leave you guys here and take Tracey home," Roger told his friends.

As Roger and I turned up the block, I took one last look over my shoulder at the Midway kids walking down the block. When I turned, I saw Chris looking at me. Our eyes met for a moment, then we both turned and headed away in our separate directions.

Suddenly, tears sprang into my eyes. "I'm really sorry, Tracey," said Roger. "I didn't mean for that to happen. Please don't be upset." His bottom lip was swollen and an ugly patch of purple and blue was forming on his right cheek.

I felt like a fool, standing there, crying. But I couldn't help it. The tears wouldn't stop. I brushed them away with the palm of my hand. "I'm sorry," I said. "I'm not really crying about the fight. Are you okay?"

"I've felt better," he admitted, wiping a trickle of blood from his lip. "I hope I'm not in big trouble on Monday. Why are you crying if it's not the fight?"

I told him about Chris and the trouble we'd been having. "That's tough," he said. "It's hard when you're both changing."

I was about to object, to say that *I* wasn't changing. Then I realized it was true. I *was* changing, too. In the beginning of the year I would never have been interested in Roger. I wouldn't have gone to Angie's by myself, either. Maybe my changes weren't as startling as Chris's, but I wasn't the same as I had been, either.

"So, I guess this was the worst first date in history," said Roger, laughing grimly.

"No, it wasn't," I said. "It was certainly exciting."

Roger stopped walking. "Are you sure?" he asked. "I'm really sorry about what happened."

"It wasn't your fault," I said. "You couldn't stand there and let Stewart take a beating."

"No. Stewart's always been a good friend," said Roger. "I'm glad you understand."

As I looked up at Roger's bruised face I thought I would melt. It seemed impossible that he could look so handsome even with his face all banged up.

The next thing that happened seemed so natural. Roger held me gently on the shoulders and kissed me on the lips.

My heart seemed to stop beating. Maybe I even stopped breathing. The smell of him, his touch, were all I knew.

When the kiss stopped, Roger looked at me and put his hand to his mouth. "Sorry for kissing you with a bloody lip," he said with a gentle smile.

I smiled back. "That's okay." He took my hand and we headed on down the block.

What a day this had turned out to be! I experienced my first kiss. And I ended the most important friendship of my life. Somehow, when I took that last glance at Chris, I knew that there was no turning back. Nothing would ever be the same between us again.

CHAPTER 9

February passed by quickly and so did March. Just as I had thought, Chris and I didn't patch up our friendship. We simply avoided one another.

When we passed in the halls or saw each other in class we would nod or say a mumbly kind of hello. It was awkward and uncomfortable.

One time I was standing on the lunch line and I hadn't noticed that Chris was only three people ahead of me. Then those three kids suddenly cut out of line to go talk to a friend. I had to move up right behind Chris!

"Hi. How's it going?" she muttered, avoiding my eyes.

"Okay," I said. "How about you?"

"Fine. No problems." There was a long pause.

Both of us fidgeted.

"We tied for first place in volleyball," I said, desperate for something to talk about.

"Great," she replied, sounding totally uninterested. Another long pause followed. "You still seeing that guy you were with at St. Luke's?" she asked.

"Yeah." Not long ago I would have wanted to tell her all about Roger. Now it seemed like none of her business.

"He's cute," she commented.

"Thanks." He's even cuter when he's not being punched by your boyfriend, I thought bitterly.

There was another awkward silence. I couldn't take it anymore. "Darn," I said, fishing through my pockets. "I forgot my money. I'll have to borrow some from Angie."

"I have money," said Chris.

"No, it's okay. Angie owes me money anyway." All this was a lie, an excuse to get off line. "See ya," I said as I left.

"Yeah. I'll see ya," she replied, seeming relieved that I was going.

As I crossed the cafeteria, I was amazed at how unconnected to Chris I'd grown. At one time I thought I would wither away and die if I didn't have Chris as my best friend. But I didn't wither away. Neither did she.

Sure, it hurt. On the day of the fight at St. Luke's, a lot of things had happened at once. That evening I was too excited about Roger to miss Chris much.

It was later that the sad, sickening feeling set in. My anger melted into a kind of horrible pain in my stomach. One night I felt so awful that I lay on my bed and sobbed until Connie came in to see what was wrong.

"That's just the way it goes sometimes," Connie said, putting her arm around my shoulders. "I'm no longer friends with any of the kids I hung out with in grammar school."

She was being kind, but I knew she didn't understand. She'd never had a best friend like Chris.

Gradually, I missed Chris less and less. And I sure didn't miss going to the mall. Roger took up a lot of my time, and so did my friendship with Angie.

When the weather got nicer, Angie began teaching me how to play tennis. Once I stopped getting blisters from the racket, I became pretty good at it. We'd go to the town courts at least twice a week after school. Angie and I had decided to join the tennis team at the end of March.

"Dynamite backhand shots!" Angie complimented me one day after we'd had a particularly long rally. "It's great having a friend who likes sports as much as I do. So many girls just want to hang out and really do nothing."

"I know what you mean," I replied honestly.

She knelt and tied her sneaker. "If you and Roger ever break up or anything, I want us to stay friends. Okay?" she said.

"Me, too," I replied.

Angie stood and flipped her long dark braid over her shoulder. "Good," she said, smiling. "I don't think I could find another friend who played both a mean game of pool *and* tennis."

I liked Angie. It was wonderful having a friend who appreciated me as I was. It was such a relief after spending the last months with Chris, who was always trying to improve me.

But even though Angie and I had lots in common, she didn't become my new best friend. We never got on exactly the same wavelength the way Chris and I had once been. I don't know why it was never like that between Angie and me. Best-friendship is almost as mysterious as romance, I suppose.

My hair slowly returned to its natural color. After a couple of haircuts almost all the coppery red was gone. I was glad. It meant I could let my own color grow all the way out, and didn't have to keep cutting it anymore. My plan was to grow my hair really long.

I kept insisting I just wanted long hair, but the truth was that Roger had mentioned that he liked long hair on girls. I wasn't going to change my whole self to please him, but I *did* want him to think I was pretty. Plus, I happen to think long hair looks cool, anyway.

Roger never asked me to change anything about myself. He seemed to like me just the way I was. We kept on seeing one another. My parents didn't exactly allow me to date him, but as long as we went out in a group in the evening, or saw one another alone during the day, they didn't complain.

At least not too much.

So things settled into a kind of calmness— until one day in the middle of May.

I was hurrying to homeroom and I passed David Madison's locker on my way. I saw a girl standing by the locker talking to David. And it wasn't Chris!

It was Kim!

They weren't just talking, either. David was kissing her. And I mean *kissing* her. Right there in the hallway!

I hadn't talked to Chris lately. But just the day before I had seen her holding hands with David in the cafeteria. They were definitely still a couple, or at least they seemed to be.

Forget it, I told myself. This is none of my business. Chris and I hadn't spoken in months. For all I knew, Chris might know about Kim already.

All morning I tried to push the thought of Kim and David out of my mind. Still, I felt an old reflex, left over from years of friendship, to want to help Chris if she was about to be hurt.

At lunch I sat with Angie and some other girls in the cafeteria. Angie was telling a funny story about one of our teachers, but I barely listened.

I was watching Chris. She was sitting with her friends, but I could tell she was looking for David. I checked Kim's usual table. She wasn't there, either.

Chris's big eyes wore a worried expression. She seemed to sense something was wrong.

I couldn't take seeing her look that way. I had to tell her what I knew.

"I'll be right back," I said to my friends as I got up.

I approached Chris's table with a tense knot in my stomach. I didn't know if I was doing the right thing, and I wasn't sure how Chris would take it. She might be angry with me, or maybe she would think I was lying. But I had to take the chance. I didn't really have anything to lose.

"Chris, hi," I said.

She seemed startled that I was speaking to her.

"Can I talk to you about something for a minute?" I continued. "Alone, I mean."

Chris's brows knit into a scowl. I could tell she was reluctant to leave the table. She was probably worried about missing David if he showed up. With a quick glance toward the door, she got up. "Okay, let's go to the girls' room," she said.

Toward the beginning of lunch the girls' room was usually pretty empty. Today it was deserted. "Chris, I'm going to tell you something because I think you should know," I began, leaning up against the aqua tile.

"Tracey, if you're going to yell at me about all the things that went wrong with our friendship, you picked a bad time," she began. "Besides, it's kind of old news, don't you think?"

That felt like a slap in the face and it made me mad. "Forget it, then," I said, heading for the door. "And that wasn't what I wanted to tell you."

Chris grabbed my arm. "I'm sorry," she said. "I was just worried you were going to tell me off, and I can't handle that today."

"Why?" I asked. "What's wrong?"

"It's David," Chris admitted. Her heavily lined eyes became misty. "He's been acting weird lately and I don't know why."

"I know why," I told her glumly.

Chris's face went ashen. "You do?"

I nodded. "I saw him with Kim in the hall-way this morning," I blurted.

Chris took a step back as if I had hit her. "What do you mean he was *with* her?" she asked.

"You know, he was definitely *with* her," I said, wanting to spare her the details.

"Was he, like . . . holding her hand?" Chris asked cautiously.

"Something like that," I admitted.

I thought that Chris was about to cry, but she surprised me. Abruptly, she folded her arms. "You're just saying these things to hurt me," she accused angrily. "It's not true."

"I wouldn't do that, Chris," I said levelly. "I hope you know me better than that."

"All I know is that this is the meanest trick anyone has ever pulled on me," she yelled. "I can't believe I almost fell for it. I'm getting out of here. David is probably sitting at the table right now, wondering where I am."

Sweeping past me, she yanked open the door. But she had only one foot in the hall when she quickly turned back, slamming the door behind her. If I thought she was ashen before, she was now dead white. It looked as though she might faint.

"What? What is it?" I asked.

Hot tears flowed down her cheeks, forming rivers of black mascara. "It . . . it's . . . them," she said in a choked voice. "They were standing in the hall . . . kissing."

Sliding down the cool tile wall, Chris sat on the floor, burying her face in the crook of her arm. I wanted so badly to say something that would take the pain away, but there was nothing to say.

Personally, I wasn't at all shocked that this had happened. I always had the feeling that David was hoping to get Kim back. Just last week I'd heard that Kim and her new boyfriend, Paul, had split up. I should have realized what was coming next.

Apparently Chris hadn't seen any of this coming. I guess she didn't want to see it. Now she had no choice.

After a while, Chris went to the sink and threw water on her puffy, red face. "It's bad enough to lose him, you know," she said, wiping her face on a rough, beige paper towel. "But besides that, now I look like such an idiot. Everyone will be saying, 'Poor Chris. David dumped her as soon as Kim came back.' You know what? I bet David was only using me all along just to make Kim jealous." This last idea made Chris start crying all over again. "What a jerk I am. A total jerk," she sobbed. "I wonder how many other people know about this."

I imagined that at least a few others had to

know. I wasn't the only person in the hallway that morning. "You were the only one who cared enough to come and tell me," said Chris. "The only one with enough guts."

Sometimes I amaze even myself. As I stood there, a brilliant idea came zooming into my head. "Look, Chris," I said. "I just had an idea that might help a little bit. It won't get you and David back together, but maybe it will help your pride some."

"What?" She sniffed.

I told her my idea and she agreed to it. "Do you think you can stay out of sight for the next few hours?" I asked.

"Sure. I'm going down to the nurse and tell her I'm sick. I honestly feel sick. She'll let me lie down or send me home."

"Good," I said. "Leave the rest to me."

Back in the cafeteria, I searched the crowd of kids until I found the person I was looking for—Patty Handleman. I spotted her talking to three of her friends. "Patty," I said, trying to sound worried. "Have you seen Chris?"

"She was here before. I don't know where she went." Patty studied my face. "Is something the matter?"

I sighed deeply. "I'm worried about her. She called me last night and said she was going to break up with David today. She's wanted to do it for weeks, but she just couldn't hurt him like that. I think she might be writing him a note right now. But I know this is hard on her. She's such a sensitive person, she hates to hurt anyone's feelings."

"Gee, that's too bad," said Patty. "I thought she was really nuts about David."

"No, that was just a front," I said knowingly. I leaned in close and half-whispered, "The truth is, Chris thought David was a little b-o-r-i-n-g."

Patty squinted her eyes and nodded. "I've always thought that myself," she admitted. "Well, if there's anything I can do, let me know."

"Actually, Patty, there is a little something," I said. "I don't know her other friends very well, so I feel funny talking to them. Could you find out if they've seen her and tell them what the problem is?"

"I can ask Phyllis," said Patty. "I see her over there."

"That would be great," I said. "Thanks."

Phase one of my plan was complete. Telling Patty this news was the surest way to spread it around. Once Patty got it to Phyllis, I knew it would travel fast. Now everyone would think that Chris had been planning to break up with David anyway.

Phase two was even easier. I went to the typing room and asked to use one of the word processors. Ms. Harris, the typing teacher, was alone grading papers. She said it would be all right.

My mother has a word processor at home, so I knew how to use one. In a second the screen was up and I began writing my letter.

> Dear David,
>
> There is no easy way to say this. I don't think we are right for one another. It's best if we call it quits and break up. Maybe you should try to get back with Kim. The two of you deserve to be together. I'll never forget you, but this relationship is no longer making me happy. I hope you understand.
>
> Your friend,

There! Brilliant! I printed the letter. For the final touch, I forged Chris's name and signed the letter. Chris and I had practiced forging one another's signatures lots of times, just for the fun of it.

I ran up to David's locker. Fortunately, he wasn't around. I slipped the letter in his locker. Done.

Around supper time that night the phone rang. "It's Chris," said my father, handing me the phone. "I haven't heard her voice in a while."

"How are you feeling?" I asked her.

"Okay, I guess," she answered. "I'm calling to thank you for what you did. Everyone's been calling me because they heard *I* broke up with David. I just got off the phone with him. He said my note was very nice but he wanted to know if the part about him and Kim deserving one another was a dig. I told him it wasn't."

A small laugh escaped my lips. "Actually, it was kind of a dig," I told her.

"I know it was," she said, laughing. "So, thanks. It helps not to look like a pathetic, dumped girlfriend."

"No problem," I said.

There was an uncomfortable silence. Neither of us knew what to say next. "Hey, it's your birthday next week," Chris said after a moment. "You'll officially be a teenager."

"Yep," I said. "I finally made it."

"If you want, maybe we can get together. I'll buy you an ice cream or something to celebrate your birthday."

"Maybe," I said. "I'm not sure what my plans are next week."

"Okay," she said. "Well, bye. And thanks."

"Bye." Gently, I hung up the phone. I didn't know how I felt. I wasn't sure I wanted to be friends with Chris again.

CHAPTER 10

Things between Chris and me were never the same. But our friendship didn't end, either. It changed.

Eventually she got over being dumped by David. It wasn't long before she was dating a cute ninth grader named Tony, who also hung around with her new friends. Except for no longer being David's girlfriend, everything stayed pretty much the same for Chris.

But for me, things kept changing.

Between volleyball and tennis, I made lots of new friends. Angie and I had both made the tennis team. Now we spent most of our time in a group with other kids who were into sports. I liked these new friends a lot. There was always something happening.

Roger took up the rest of my time. Luckily, though, he was very involved with sports at St. Luke's, so there was no conflict about how much time we spent together. He understood that I had a busy schedule, and I understood the same about him.

It was one of the zillion things I liked about him. He was interested in so many things that he wasn't just moping around waiting for me all the time. That would have driven me bonkers.

Somehow—between sports, new friends, and Roger—I squeezed in my homework. Don't ask me how, but I did.

What happened to my friendship with Chris? I made up my mind that Chris and I had nothing in common. I passed on letting her buy me a birthday ice cream. I told her I was too busy. I figured if the friendship was over, I might as well just forget about it. There was no sense hanging onto the past anymore.

But one day, toward the end of May, Chris changed my mind.

I had stayed after school to attend a meeting of the Sports Club. I was thinking of joining next year.

After the meeting was over, Angie, a girl

named Carol, and I were crossing the school-yard, heading toward the back gate. We were planning to go to the Greatdale Diner to pig out on shakes and fries.

Suddenly, I heard Chris call out to me. I turned and saw her with a group of friends. They were all hanging around—looking cool—leaning up against the school.

"Tracey!" she called again, waving.

I waved back. Chris left her friends and hurried toward me.

"What does *she* want?" mumbled Angie, who never did like Chris.

I shrugged. "Beats me. You guys go ahead. I'll meet you at the diner," I said.

"Okay," said Carol as she and Angie kept on walking.

"Hi," said Chris breathlessly when she reached me. I saw that she had a new hairdo. It was cut really short on the sides and fell down in long bangs to the top of her lined eyes. Her hair color was an even whiter blond. By now, none of this seemed at all peculiar to me. I was used to the way Chris looked.

"What are you doing tonight?" she asked, digging around in the neon-striped canvas bag slung over her shoulder.

"I'm going to the diner now. After that, nothing," I said.

Chris pulled a black video box from her bag and presented it to me proudly. "Take a look at that!" she said.

"*Make-Up Secrets of the Rock Stars*," I read from the label on the spine.

"Oops." She giggled, snatching the video away from me. "That's the wrong one." After more digging, she handed me another video.

"Where did you get this?" I gasped when I read the title. *The Johnny Dupré Collection: Greatest Moments*. It was a collection of the best scenes from all of Johnny Dupré's movies. It had never been in the theater, I was sure of that. I'd never even heard of it.

"Tony's brother owns a video store," she explained. "I was there when it came in, so I had to rent it immediately. I knew you would go berserk when you saw it. It just went on the shelf this morning."

"This is awesome!" I cried.

"I was thinking that maybe we could watch it together," Chris suggested cautiously. Was she making one last effort to save our friendship? It sure looked that way. How could I be stubborn in the face of that? "Okay," I said. "Do you want to come over around seven?"

"Sounds cool," Chris said, her face breaking into that wide, bright smile that no amount of make-up could change.

That evening Chris came over. At first, things were strained. We didn't quite know how to have an easy conversation anymore. Then we put the tape in and everything changed. We were laughing and shouting, or squealing with delicious terror, depending on what was happening.

"I remember this scene. It's from *Surfside Slug Monsters!*" Chris said, pounding my arm. "This is my favorite."

It was like old times.

When the tape ended, we went into the kitchen and raided the freezer. As we sat with our bowls of ice cream, we didn't have any in-depth talk about our friendship. We just gossiped about people we knew and laughed over funny things that had happened in school.

In a way, it was better that we now had different friends and did different things. We had more to talk about.

Shortly after Chris left, Roger called me. He called almost every night if we didn't see one another. I realized how happy and excited I was as I told him how I had spent my evening. I was glad Chris and I had patched things up. I hadn't realized how much I'd missed her.

"That sounds great," he said. Another thing I love about Roger is that he's always really happy when good things happen to me. "Do you think you two will go back to being best friends?"

"I don't think so," I said. "I'm not sure what's going to happen."

Here's what happened.

Every couple of weeks or so, Chris and I get together to watch a video. Sometimes they're horror videos, which I pick. Other times they're romances, which she picks. Some of those I really like; most of them I suffer through since it's only fair.

I never hang out with her friends. She never hangs out with mine. But when we see each other, we have fun. Maybe we're not best friends anymore, but our friendship is strong. We both know it's going to last.

As I said in the beginning, some changes you see coming. Others just sneak up on you. Either way, I've learned that, like it or not, life keeps on changing and changing again. All you can do is keep adjusting to the changes.

And maybe if you're lucky, like Chris and I, you can save the best of the old as you move ahead to the new.